The Stupid Things We Did When We Were Kids.

Steve Beed

Copyright 2025©Steve Beed
All rights reserved
ISBN: 9798300814878

To Annie.

Acknowledgements

All characters and events in this book are fictitious; any similarity to persons living or dead is coincidental.

The setting of the book is based on the town of Exmouth, where I grew up. I have taken terrible liberties with the geography of the town, for which I make no apologies.

A BEGINNING

My work regularly brings me to a city close to this small coastal town, near enough for me to come and spend an hour or so here before embarking on the long journey back to my family. I don't think my wife, Claire, knows I still come here. If she does, she is diplomatic enough not to mention it. I don't lie to her, I just don't tell her. I am always truthful and honest with my wife, which makes this omission unusual. Unusual, yes, unique, no - there is another thing I have never told her, a thing so awful I will never allow myself to share it. She doesn't know about the summer of 1976. Maybe I've told her some of it, but not everything.

Each time I come here – I think of it as 'coming home' although it's decades since I've lived here - I follow the same routine. Firstly, I park in the road I grew up in. This gets progressively more difficult each year as the quantity and size of the cars increase, lined up outside the houses and in front gardens that have been converted to driveways. The road is no longer the playground of my childhood. It is now a busy cut-through for impatient drivers who tend to go just a bit too fast. I walk past my parents' old house. It's a long time since they lived there, and a cursory glance is all that is needed for me to remind myself what it looks like. There's fresh paint, different curtains, newer cars outside on a bed of gravel – but at its heart, it's the same old two-storey red-brick house with my old bedroom window looking out over the road.

Once I have completed this part of the ritual, I walk down through the town. The long road with shops and homes interspersed at regular intervals has changed many times through the intervening years. The toy shop, a treasure trove of my childhood, became a bike shop, then a pet shop, and most recently, a delightfully aromatic pizza place. A small handful of shops have stayed resiliently true to their original incarnations, but most of the route is now unfamiliar to me. Some of my memories of the town have grown vague as the years have passed, but my recall of the feel of it is deeply ingrained: sand, seagulls, salty air and friendships forged in the carefree, halcyon days of childhood – the Shangri-la of a perfect pre-adolescence. The town has changed – but it still feels like home, the bones are still the same.

The end of the main road offers a choice. You can cut through the shopping arcade – built in the late 1970s and now looking as faded and tired as the buildings it replaced, or turn right towards the estuary, which hugs one side of the town. The town and river are stitched together by a railway track that leads back to the city.

I take the estuary route, wending my way towards the mud flats and open water. Here, wading birds feed with one wary eye out as the cyclists and the walkers - with their noisy, excitable dogs, promenade along the newly completed scenic walkway and cycle route. I don't join them on the path through the waist-high foliage and scrubland, that's definitely not for me. For now, I turn South in the direction of the sea.

I pass the gleaming white boats that jostle for space in the marina. The square of water that used to be a working dock when I was a boy, full of fishing boats and burly men with faded tattoos unloading stinking fish meal and replacing it with billowing clouds of china clay. Before that, it was a launching pad for many of Sir Walter Raliegh's Elizabethan voyages, or so I was told. Now, it is full of the expensive toys of the people who visit when their busy schedules allow. They stay in the luxury flats that have been built around the area, all clean lines and modern amenities. I leave them behind me when I arrive at the junction of the river and the channel, which is where I finally stop and sit on a low stone wall. This is the place where I will contemplate and, inevitably, question my decision to return here once more. This town is haunted by the ghosts of the kids I grew up with, the friends who shared the first chapter of my life but are now consigned to history and fading memories.

On previous visits, I have sat here alone after walking through an almost deserted town centre. I have visited in fog so thick that you only know the sea is there because of the sound of the waves and the gentle, rhythmic, metallic clanking of rigging against the masts of the boats moored nearby. There has been apocalyptic rain that has soaked through every layer of clothing I am wearing. Gales strong enough to throw stinging sand into my face, even when I am up on the road. Sometimes, I come here on winter evenings when it is nearly dark. I look across at the distant lights of the small villages on the far bank as dusk arrives. The times that best match my feelings on these return visits are when I have sat under flat grey skies, watching gulls apathetically circle in the overcast sky.

Today is not any one of those days. I drove here with the aircon on full, I left my jacket and tie in the car, and still felt vastly overdressed for the blast-furnace heat of the afternoon sun. I make it to my customary spot with my shirt sticking to my body at the front and back, my feet starting to slip and slide inside my brown leather work shoes. I sit on the wall and take a long drink from the bottle of water that I had the foresight to buy on my way past the shops, but it is half gone before I even feel it start to refresh me. To my left, the beach is still thronging with families, to my right, two men with boats on trailers are vying for space with one another on the slipway. I watch as the men, in shorts and flip-flops, argue about whose 4x4 has the right of way, their voices raised and tempers short. I feel sympathy for both of them. All they want is to get out on the water to enjoy the last part of a glorious day. All they want is to be able to go about their own business without anything, or anyone, getting in their way.

I tell myself I don't know why I'm here. Why I keep coming back to this place, even though I have no reason to visit now – apart from a desire to reconnect with a past that I couldn't wait to leave behind. I tell myself that, but deep inside, I'm sure I do know.

I'm certain it's the heat of the day, the hot, humid feel under the glare of the sun, that triggers the memories. I have my reasons for why I keep returning, like the prodigal son, at regular intervals for all these years. They are not reasons I can easily explain, but I do not come to remember the town or the people. I come to remember that summer. A deep-rooted need to try and make sense of what happened has driven me to keep coming here, to look for answers that I know will be elusive, although today feels different, it feels as though they might just be within reach.

ONE

The radio was playing in the deserted kitchen when I came downstairs, not Ed Stewpot's Junior Choice, which I had barely grown out of, but an ebullient Tony Blackburn. Elton John promised not to break Kiki Dee's heart while I poured some cornflakes into a bowl with the last of the milk. I ate it as I wandered through the downstairs rooms, slopping splashes of milk onto the carpet, checking to see who was in. Each room I looked into was as devoid of life as the last, so I trailed back into the kitchen to dump my bowl in the already crowded sink. As I dropped it in, I noticed the list next to the kettle. Written in my mum's familiar, swirling handwriting on a page torn from her notebook. For a moment, I thought I might pretend I hadn't noticed it, but I knew from bitter experience that would not wash. There would be hell to pay in the evening, plus the jobs would simply roll over onto tomorrow's list - and be extended.

I picked up the piece of paper as Mr Blackburn helpfully informed me that it was going to be hot today. He sounded inordinately cheerful about it, although it's hardly surprising news; it's been hot forever. Or at least it had been since June when I had to sit in sweltering classrooms with the windows open, the heat of the day imploring me to go outside and have fun. I guess it's probably a good thing now, considering that I am on my summer holiday at last. I read the list:

*'I had to go out, please can you walk the dog, wash the   dishes and pop*out *and get some more milk and a loaf of bread? Thanks love, Mum. X'*

I briefly wondered where she had to go so urgently that she couldn't even turn off the radio. I don't know what Mum does most of the time when I'm at school. I know she does laundry at a local boarding school, but that should be closed now it's the summer. Maybe she still has to go in and do the nun's washing for them, who knows? I shrugged to myself, then looked out of the window into the garden. Max was in the middle of the lawn, he stopped scratching at the grass and looked up at me, wagging his tail expectantly. I let out a sigh, feeling that this was an unfair imposition on my time, even though he was my dog, and I had nothing else to do. I jabbed the off button, silencing the radio as Abba launched into Dancing Queen, then stomped off upstairs to get my jeans and trainers on.

While I was dressing, I ruminated on the list; the dishes would probably wait, and nobody would need anything clean until teatime. Similarly, the shopping wasn't urgent as it would be ages before anyone else was home. This decided it then, I would take the dog to the park.

Glad to have made a decision, I got the lead from the hook by the door and collected Max from the garden. The park is close to home, it's enormous, with huge areas of grass, massive trees – ideal for climbing, and a play area for smaller children. At one corner there is an old railway embankment leading to the disused viaduct, which looms majestically over this part of the town. There is a small pond that used to be a boating lake and is now a morass of duckweed. In other words, the park is a kid's paradise. I unclipped the lead as I walked through the gate, watching as Max ran a short distance ahead before following him into the park.

The kiddie's play park, with its brightly painted swings and slides, was, predictably, full of younger kids being supervised by a mixture of parents and older siblings, this was not the place for me. But on the far side of the deserted tennis courts, I could hear voices, laughing, shouting and whooping. I walked in the direction of the sounds, with Max hurrying to catch up when he realised that I'd altered my course. As I approached, I saw a group of boys and girls my age and upwards. I recognised some of them from school, although not well enough to know their names or where they lived.

In my mind's eye, they were dangling from tree branches, doing stunts, shooting homemade bows and arrows and fighting with sticks – like a deleted scene from Lord of the Flies. In reality, it was half a dozen boys, four bikes and a couple of girls sitting on the grass nearby, pretending to take no notice of them. The boys were cycling up and down the dust-dry mud banks on the waist-high mound between the trees, some riding solo, others standing perilously on the backs of bikes while the riders attempted to traverse the trail without overbalancing or colliding with the tree trunks. The bank ran along the edge of a steep path, which they rode back up to start again. A great deal of shouting and some exuberant swearing accompanied this activity.

Inspired, I took the shortcut that reduced the distance of the circular route that I had been instructed to take when walking Max. Delivering him back to the garden, I pulled my bike out of the shed and pedalled back to the park and the mud banks. I hesitated for a moment before joining in with gusto. While I was not as proficient as some of the bigger boys, I was no slouch when it came to cycling. I tagged along at the back, riding down through the trees, cutting across to the path with a tyre-shredding skid, which was the accepted way of stopping, before standing on the pedals to power back up the footpath and repeat the process. Everyone was trying to make it appear effortless and be more stylish than everyone else, and I was holding my own, more or less.

After my third run, I was walking back up the path with my bike after a minor knee-scraping mishap. Sweat beaded on my brow, and I was slightly out of breath, one of the big boys approached me, ginger hair cropped close to his scalp and a grubby tee shirt with a collar that looked like it had grown actual wings. I knew who he was, he was two years older than me and hung around with my friend Bert's big brother, Alan. Alan always referred to him as Tubs, but I was pretty sure that I would not be allowed to call him by that name. He was one of the kids who hadn't bought along a bike of his own and had been cadging rides off anyone who would have him. The others were trying to avoid him as his bulk made it harder to manoeuvre their bikes when he was on the back.

"You hurt your knee then?"

"Only a bit, it's okay," I lied – it really hurt, but I wasn't about to admit that in front of Tubs or the other boys.

"Can I borrow your bike while you're hurt then?"

I'm not supposed to lend my bike to people. This has been a rule for me since Mum and Dad first provided me with my own transportation, lovingly assembled from cannibalised parts of other bikes my dad had acquired. But Tubs was bigger than me.

"Yeh, okay, just one go round though."

I then stood and watched as my bike, with its new operator, proceeded to go through the trees, along the path and up and down the banks multiple times while I nursed my knee and wondered how I was going to get my bike back. I thought about going and sitting on the grass with the girls, but you know – they were girls.

I was worried that Tubs was simply going to get bored with the game and cycle off with my bike. I'd get into trouble with Dad, meaning I would never hear the last of it, and I would be doomed to a summer of the worst chores that Mum could devise for me. I tried to intersect Tubs as he went back up the path for another turn, but he grinned and swerved away, circling the girls and shouting something at them before returning to the top of the slope.

I became more certain that he intended to ride away with my bike, and a fluttering feeling of unease began to take over my stomach as I stood watching him descend the banks. I started looking around for a grown-up who might come to my aid. No such luck; the nearest adults were over by the playpark, and they wouldn't be leaving their own children to come and help me. I was just going to have to helplessly watch it happen.

Then, unexpectedly, one of the older boys shouted, "Oi, Tubs, give that kid his bike back before he cries."

"Or what?" he answered belligerently.

"Or I'll tell your sister," the bigger boy responded.

The other boys laughed, and the girls looked in my direction and giggled. I know I went bright red, and at that moment, I thought I might start to cry. But for some reason, Tubs did what the other boy had told him. He came over and dropped the bike at my feet with a crash.

"Thanks. You might need to pump that up."

He grinned and pointed at the completely flat back tyre. I knew straight away that it would need more than pumping, which meant I would have to bother Dad this evening. Because even though he had shown me how to fix punctures before, I never seemed to be able to get it right. I walked disconsolately home, pushing my clattering bike beside me, dumped it in the middle of the back garden and went inside.

The house was still empty, I messed around in my room for a bit, reading some old Commando comics and imagining myself machine-gunning Tubs in revenge for bursting my bike tyre. After finishing a story, I decided that it was probably time for lunch, or if not that, a snack. That was when I remembered I hadn't done the shopping yet, so there would be no sandwich until I'd been to get the bread. I took the money from the small purse by the front door, considered taking a bit extra for sweets, and then decided against it. Mum knew to the penny how much was in the purse and how much the shopping would come to.

The short walk to the nearest shop would've been okay, but their bread cost a few pence more than the shop in town. I had strict instructions to go to the furthest one, so that was the direction I went – more or less. I cut through as many back alleys and lanes as I could on the way, not for any particular reason other than I could. Passing garages, mysterious doors with peeling paint and rarely used back gates. These are the routes that adults rarely use, the murky hidden world behind the façade of civilisation on the roads that the front of the houses look onto. Eventually, I made it to the shop and procured a loaf of Mothers Pride and a bottle of milk, handing over my 30p and waiting for the change, which I put carefully in my pocket. The bottle was wet with condensation, making it slippery in my hand as I walked home in the heat of the midday sun, I had to juggle it with the loaf of bread whilst hoping I didn't drop either of them.

Thankfully, the milk and bread made it safely home. I put the bottle in the fridge and the change in the purse, then made myself a sandwich with the last triangle of soft cheese wrapped in foil. I sat in the kitchen and ate my lunch, washing it down with a glass of orange squash while I considered what I should do next, now that I'd practically finished my jobs for the day. After my run-in with Tubs earlier, Bert had been on my mind.

He's not really called Bert; his actual name is Robert, but when we started secondary school, our hundred-year-old maths teacher misheard him and started calling him Bert – so we all did. Most of us have different names from the ones our parents call us: Bert (my friend Robert), Hedgehog – (because it sounds like Hitchcock), Nobby (no idea), Ernie (walks with a limp because he got run over by a milk float), Brick (had a haircut that looked like a brick), Scrapsy (good at fighting). Some nicknames were just derivations of people's actual names, like Foggy, Mal, Jonesy, Smithy. Then others focussed on people's physical characteristics: Fatty, Stinky, Beaky, Wingnut and others, all equally unpleasant. Maybe that's not right, but we didn't know any better, we were just kids, after all. Anyway, I'm known as Shorts – because Mum made me wear a pair of shorts to school once when I tore my new trousers and the spare pair were in the wash. Apparently, it's funny because I'm actually quite tall for my age. I don't mind it anyway. It's better than some of the things people get called. The girls, for reasons that I have no explanation for, seemed to have mostly escaped this renaming ritual.

I started secondary school last September, a significant rite of passage for all preteens. In the years after I left, I would hear people refer to their schools, commenting on how big they were. I inwardly chuckled when they revealed that the aforementioned school had as many as 500 students. My school was bigger than that, way bigger. It was rumoured to be the biggest school in Europe at the time – although it was hard to verify information like that in those pre-internet days. I'm pretty sure there were about 500 kids just in my year group. Despite the very wide choice available to me, I have only made a few new friends since then. I don't usually like meeting new people, and there were a lot of new people.

But Bert latched on to me from the very start of term. He is really laid back, and he only lives around the corner. Halfway through the year, he started knocking on my door on his way to school. I would rush around, finding my shoes/homework/PE kit while he waited in the hallway, and then we would walk the remaining short distance together. It was better than arriving on my own, so I didn't mind. I was quite happy, in fact. Since then, we have become good friends.

Making sure I locked the door, I walked around to the next road, where Bert lived with his mum and older brother. As I approached his house, Bert was rushing out of his front door, leaving it hanging open behind him,

"Fruit lorry's here!" he announced loudly, then ran past me to the alley that ran under the viaduct behind his house, I turned and followed him. Like viaducts everywhere, the spaces under the tall brick arches were used for a variety of small businesses: a garage, a small breakers yard and some storage areas. One of these lock-ups was owned by a local fruit and veg shop owner. The veg was of little interest to us, but if we 'helped' the driver unload his truck, he would let us have the pick of any spilt fruit.

Together, we ran over and joined the swarming gang that had already descended like locusts on the lorry. Boxes were lugged, dragged, ferried, carried and stacked in the cool, dark storage area by a range of kids, both big and small. Some of the little ones were working in pairs, moving the heavy boxes, the older children gave them first choice for the smaller containers – there was enough for everyone. Under the guidance of the driver, who stood supervising proceedings with his shirt sleeves rolled up past his elbows, a cigarette in the corner of his mouth and a smile on his face, the truck was emptied, and everything we could scavenge was gone. He picked up a box of peaches and told us to take one each.

The helpers disappeared one by one as they received their reward, back to wherever they had come from. Bert and I went back to his house, eating peaches as big as our heads. I was aware that the clean clothes I had started the day in had now accumulated a range of fresh stains. Along with the dusty mud from my cycling exploits, there was peach juice, red strawberry marks where I had wiped my hands after carrying a box with some squashed contents, a spattering of some other unidentified fruit on one sleeve, and smudged black marks down the front from where we had been clambering on the lorry. I decided I could probably wipe the worst of this off with a damp cloth when I got home before Mum noticed.

After we had eaten our peaches, we messed around in Bert's garden for a bit, throwing stones into the yard over the wall to see whose would make the best/loudest noise if it hit anything. After the bloke who owned the yard yelled at us to stop, Bert found his bag of marbles from his room, and we played with them for a bit. I realised, as the day was cooling down, that it was possibly approaching time to go home. There was no fixed time for this, just an instruction to 'be home in time for tea.' We checked the clock in the front room, and confirming that it was nearly five, we made a hasty and vague arrangement to meet again the next day before I hurried off.

At home, it was triple trouble. The filthy clothes, which didn't go unnoticed, and incomplete chores were bad enough, but having to then confess to bursting my bike tyre was the icing on the cake. I was told that I needed to start acting my age. I wasn't sure how to go about that. All the kids I know are twelve, the same as me, and we all act pretty much the same. I guessed it wasn't the right time for that discussion, though. I poured a generous amount of washing-up liquid into the sink and splashed the dishes in and out while Mum made tea. We ate together, then covered Dad's mince and boiled potatoes with foil and put them in the oven to stay warm until he got home.

It had become normal to put his tea in the oven during this scorching summer. He was rarely back when his shift at the fire station was supposed to end. He has spent a lot of time on the moors and commons putting out fires since the hot weather started, doing overtime and extra shifts. When he is at home, he doesn't have the energy to do much more than sitting in his armchair with a permanent smell of bonfires enveloping him. I guessed I probably wasn't going to see him again tonight and took myself upstairs to read comics.

Sitting on my bed next to the open window, I could hear the twins from number twenty-six playing in the road. Tony and Terry Crimp are about seven or eight years old. They seem to spend most of their time shouting and playing in and around the small patch of garden at the front of their house. As dusk approached, I heard their mum calling them back inside. They were eventually corralled inside, in their absence, the sounds of birds finding an evening roost took over as I listened out for the sound of Dad's car.

TWO

The following days' list started with: DON'T MAKE A NOISE – DAD IS SLEEPING. It then gave instructions for two or three jobs that I attempted to complete in silence. I kind of blew it when I knocked Mum's blue vase off the shelf while I was wiping the dusting cloth around it, I'm not even sure why she's got it, it's not like there are ever any flowers in it. Luckily, it wasn't broken, but when Dad came downstairs to see what the noise was, he suggested (quite strongly) that I should go out and play and stop making so much racket. I didn't have to be asked twice, and I was off to Bert's before Dad had even finished picking up the vase and checking it for damage.

Bert was sitting on his front wall, apparently waiting for me. He jumped down as I arrived, his long black hair flying as his Dunlop Green Flash hit the pavement, and he started to walk beside me, away from his house. It always felt good walking with Bert, he had a swagger in his stride and seemed to talk easily to everyone. Today, he had a blue tee shirt with a crisp white collar, like the one I'd asked Mum for. She'd told me it was too dear, so I got a striped one without a collar. Instead, such is the unfairness of life.

"Where are we going?" I asked, I had taken it for granted that I was joining him in whatever it was that he had planned.

"You'll see," he answered as he gave the road a cursory glance before dashing across.

I waited for a gap in the traffic, then ran to catch up,

"What'll I see? Did you catch it last night for messing your clothes up?"

He shrugged and made a non-committal grunting sound, seemingly in answer to both questions, before making a sharp turn into an alley. He stopped and turned to face me.

"Do you know the way into the Wilds?"

It was my turn to shrug now, along with a shake of my head. The Wilds are the fenced-in overgrown area alongside the railway track. Brambles, bushes, nettles and bracken grow in abundance, towering along the edge of the fence. I knew the big kids went there but had never attempted to explore them myself.

"I do," Bert informed me, "come on, I'll show you."

He continued along the alley, and I hurried to keep up.

"Are we allowed?"

Bert laughed at this,

"Of course not, but who's going to know?"

I wasn't sure. I knew who some of the big kids who messed around in there were. Boys I did my best to stay out of the way of. Also, I had been given stern warnings from Dad about not messing about by the train tracks. The potential consequences of getting caught had been emphasised, although why it was so dangerous had never really been explained. I didn't want to get caught, but I was curious about what made it such a dangerous and forbidden place.

"So how do we get in? The fence is too high, isn't it?"

"Not here," Bert had stopped and was pointing to the bottom corner of the railings, where they adjoined the corner of a house. The fence towered over us, green flaking paint covering years of rust. Two of the metal bars, the ones tucked into the very corner, had been bent inwards at their base, creating a space big enough to crawl through. I was hesitant, but Bert crouched down and scurried straight through. I looked around to check who was watching, then, seeing nobody, I made my way to the other side.

It was a little disappointing. We were standing in a patch of bare, dry mud, where it was just as hot, dusty and uninteresting as the pavement side of the fence. Along the edge of the fence was a trail of litter, in various stages of decomposition, that had been posted through the bars by passers-by over the years. In front of us was a bank covered in blackberry bushes and waist-high ferns, Bert started to climb up an almost invisible trail that led through them. He held his arms above his head to stop them from getting scratched as he squeezed past the thorns and spikes that reached out to him. I copied him, keeping my arms above my head until I caught up with him at the summit. We stood together and looked at the vista in front of us - the Wilds.

Spread out before me was a large green, tangled triangle, covered in whatever plants had managed to find roots here over the years; Buddleias surrounded by butterflies, bracken, blackberry bushes, tall grass and patches of gorse all competed for space, creating a small jungle. From our viewpoint, I could see the fence behind us curving around to the mossy glass roof and red bricks of the train station, which marks the tip of the triangle. There are some rusted, disused railway tracks, like scars from long ago when the station was busier. They lead in the general direction of the broken end of the old viaduct. Coming out of the station is a raised bank, with train tracks resting on the top, it forms a barrier that separates the wilds from the estuary. Away to my right, signifying the end of the Wilds, there is a brook that carries the town's drain water into the edge of the river mouth via a short tunnel under the train tracks.

Most of the plants here are a faded, dusty, green colour, dried out by the weeks of sunshine and a nearly total absence of rain in the last few months. The whispering of insects and the salt smell of the estuary give the place an unworldly, ethereal feel, far away from the murmuring traffic and busy streets. I can sense that there is something special about this secret place, it is hidden and devoid of any signs of adult interference. I am glad that Bert has brought me here. I take it all in as I stand in the bright sunshine, side by side with my friend.

He turned and grinned at me, and just for a moment, I caught a glimpse of an older person – the confident, successful man I was certain he would become. I wondered for a moment what it would be like to be him, and then he broke the silence, "Well, what do you think Shorts?" he made it sound as if he was trying to sell it to me.

"It's fab," I answer.

"That's the Grotty Grotto," he tells me, pointing to a circular patch that is a different shade of yellowing green in the centre of the area.

"Eh?" I can see what he is showing me, but I have no idea what a Grotty Grotto is.

"It's where they hang out, nobody can see them in there. They can do what they like." He looks at me knowingly, but I have no idea what sort of things he is alluding to.

"C'mon," he started to walk along the ridge of the bank, following another near-invisible path through the foliage. I stepped tentatively behind him on the loose, dusty path. I was looking at my feet and nearly walked into him as he stopped in front of a large concrete cube. It is about ten feet tall with a rusted green padlocked door. A peeling yellow sticker bears the warning 'DANGER – ELECTRICITY'. Underneath this, someone has scrawled 'THE BUNKER' in large, capital chalk letters.

Together, we walked around its perimeter. There was nothing to see apart from a few names scratched into its surface with stones – TESSA LOVES IAN, inside a crudely drawn heart - and some cracked and damaged areas on its corners. We got back to the door, and Bert boosted himself onto one of the oversized hinges and pulled himself up onto the roof.

"What are you doing?" I ask.

"What does it look like? C'mon, are you coming up or not?"

"It says danger."

"I'm alright, aren't I?"

I had to bend my neck to look up at Bert now. The roof seemed impossibly high from where I was standing, but I didn't want Bert to think I was a wimp. I hesitantly set one of my plimsolls on the hinge and pushed myself upwards until my fingers reached the edge of the roof, then I scrambled gracelessly up to join Bert. I'm not sure why we bothered, everything looked pretty much the same as it did from the bank. The main difference is that we could now see into the Grotty Grotto, it was a circle of bare earth with a blackened bull's eye at its centre. A selection of milk crates and a generous distribution of litter surrounded the fire pit, evidence of the regular visits of the older kids.

I looked down at the base of our perch, and a brief feeling of nausea rose in me, causing me to take an involuntary step back from the edge.

"How do we get down?" I ask.

"Like this," Bert replied with a grin. To my horror, he then stepped forward and, whooping, launched himself over the edge. I looked over in time to see him land in a large patch of bracken, which he had crushed as he rolled over before getting to his feet and brushing himself off. He looked up at me expectantly.

"Your turn."

I looked down and knew that I couldn't do it, it was too high. Instead, I sat on the edge and turned and lowered myself down the wall until my arms were at full stretch before letting myself drop for the last couple of feet. Even from that small height, I managed to fall backwards onto my bum. I looked up, and Bert was standing over me, proffering his outstretched hand, I took it, and he helped me back to my feet, grinning all the time.

"We'll both jump next time, yeah? The ferns are really soft when you land in them."

I wasn't sure that I would, but I agreed anyway, "Sure."

"Let's go and see the Grotto."

We went towards the centre of the wilds, following another hidden trail until we emerged into the Grotty Grotto. It was a disappointment, just as grubby and bare as it had looked from the top of the bunker. I looked back, but this area must have been in a dip. By some strange quirk, I couldn't see the concrete cube at all from down here. Bert kicked up a cloud of dust, then went and sat on one of the crates. I sat on another, and we looked at the empty cans, crisp packets, and cigarette ends spread around the ground.

"Do they smoke here? The big kids."

"Yeah, they drink too," answered Bert, pointing at an empty beer can like the ones my dad has sometimes. "Girls come here too," he added, looking at me in a knowing way that I found hard to give any meaning to.

"You know?" he added and started kissing the back of his hand. He looked up at me and started laughing and pulling a face that indicated what a low opinion he had of that activity. I laughed with him. Abruptly, he stopped and reached down into the dust at his feet.

"Look!" he exclaimed, holding out two coins that he had just plucked from the ground," they must have fallen out of someone's pocket. You know what this means, don't you?"

"Penny chews?" I speculated.

"Pillock, no look."

I looked properly and saw that it was two of the big, old pennies, the ones that kids threw at each other, and you couldn't spend in the shops any more.

"C'mon, you'll see."

With that, he was off again, practically running along another hidden path with me hurrying after him.

"Where are we going?"

I got no answer but didn't have to wait long to find out; we arrived at the taller bushes that lined the edge of the train track. As I caught up with Bert, he pushed his way through them and scrambled up the gravel bank to the lines. I watched in horror as he laid his head on the track closest to us.

"What are you bloody doing?" I called from the bottom of the bank.

"Listening for trains coming, it's how you do it. I saw it on the Lone Ranger."

"Eh?"

"You put your ear on the track, and you can hear it coming."

"You'd hear it anyway, they're really big and noisy."

"I suppose," he slid back down the slope and stood beside me. As he reached my side as if on cue, we both heard the sound of the approaching train in the distance. We looked up from the bushes and saw it coming into view, then bearing down on the final straight stretch that led into the station. We watched the metal leviathan from the bushes as it rushed past us, with its wheels screeching against the metal tracks. The engine roared, and waves of heat wafted towards us in its wake. I looked over at Bert. He was leaning forward with his long, straight hair blowing backwards in the draft and a beaming smile on his face. As it passed us, the train started to slow down in readiness for the end of its journey. It crawled into the station, where it finally came to a squealing, rattling halt.

"Right," said Bert, "now."

He passed one of the pennies to me and scaled the bank again, at the top, he turned and motioned for me to follow him.

"What are we doing?" I asked as I moved forward.

"Put it on the track like this." He placed his coin on the hot metal train track and waited for me to do the same. Once I had, he looked back at the station and then turned to me.

"Now we wait for the train to come back," he offered, "back into the bushes."

Being an estuary, this is the end of the line for the train. Once it gets to the station, the passengers on board are exchanged for the ones on the platform, and the train goes back in the direction it has just come from. We waited in the bushes and watched as the activity on the platform started to dwindle and the train got ready to depart. A distant whistle told us it was on its way, and we peered up to see it slowly building up speed as it clanked and clattered past us in an envelope of noise and smell.

As soon as it had passed, Bert was scrambling back up to the track, where he proudly held up two squashed and misshapen coins. I took the one he offered me; it was still warm. We sat in the sun and examined them together. The details had been distorted, obscuring the edges, which had become sharpened and uneven. He put his in his pocket.

"We should keep these," he said, "for luck."

I agreed, putting my own in my pocket and making sure it was pushed all the way down. I was certain I could already feel the luck radiating from it, I didn't want to lose it so soon after I had acquired it. We both looked up as we heard distant voices, shouts and laughter. We peered across to the far side of the Wilds, where I could see the foliage moving as unseen bodies passed through it.

"Big kids," I whispered.

"It's Alan and his stupid mates," Bert replied in the same hushed tones, "I can hear his voice."

I wasn't sure that we needed to keep our voices low, we were some distance away from them for now. Also, they were making so much racket as they crashed through the undergrowth that I was pretty certain they wouldn't have heard us even if we'd been yelling. Even so, I continued to talk in a quiet voice, "How do we get out? We can't get past them."

I didn't want to think about what might happen if we tried to go back the way we came, we were almost certain to get pushed into the thorns – or worse.

"We can go this way," Bert pointed up the tracks. I must have looked doubtful because he continued, "We can go across the brook."

I looked once more at the advancing troop of older children; they still hadn't seen us, and I wanted it to stay that way. I resigned myself to getting wet shoes and followed Bert as he clambered through the shrubs along the edge of the slope.

I needn't have worried about getting my feet wet. When we got to the brook, it was barely a trickle. Normally, it would be halfway to your knees and ten feet wide here, but after weeks of sun and no rain, it had been reduced to an easily traversable stream with cracked and flaking mud along its banks.

Pleased with ourselves for managing to slip away, we started the long, hot walk back.

"What are you doing this evening?" I asked.

"Dunno, probably just watch telly. What about you?"

I felt a pang of jealousy. Our telly had gone back to Radio Rentals for the summer. Mum said it was because she didn't want me sitting around watching it all day while she was at work. I knew that it was also because we were skint most of the time. I mostly felt aggrieved because I knew that her regular trips to visit Auntie Jean in the evenings were carefully timed to coincide with Crossroads, it didn't seem fair.

"I'm just going to read some comics, what about tomorrow?"

"I'll call round for you; we can go swimming."

"I'm skint."

"Me too, I meant at the beach, in the sea."

"I'm not meant to without Mum or Dad there."

"They won't know though, will they? I'll call round about eleven."

I didn't want to say no, I was glad that Bert wanted to spend time with me, so I agreed. We parted company at the end of his road with shouts of 'see you tomorrow'. I walked home holding the flattened penny in my pocket, feeling it smooth and warm in the palm of my hand, leeching its good luck into my pores through the barrier of mud and grime.

THREE

The doorbell rang a few minutes after I had finished racing through my morning list, hanging the washing out, walking Max, and then clearing up his dog logs from the back garden. I let Bert inside, where he waited in the hallway while I went and looked for my swimming trunks and a towel. Once I was fully equipped, we left the house and started the walk through town to the beach.

Normally, we would cut through the backways like I did yesterday. I knew them like the back of my hand, I had been walking myself to and from school since I was eight, giving me plenty of time to explore. But Bert's mum had given him some money for the swimming pool when she saw he had his trunks rolled in a towel and ready. He was going to buy some sweets we could share out for our lunch. I had filled an old squash bottle with some water, the inch or so of cordial left in the bottle would make it palatable, and found half a packet of digestive biscuits in the cupboard – so we were set up for the day.

We went through town via the newsagents, then past the town centre and up around the fountain. We turned down the shaded walkway that cut through behind the big hotel. By the time we reached the seafront, I was baked, as ready for a swim as I would ever be. I stood by the sea wall, looking for a space on the crowded sand, covered in windbreaks, deck chairs and towels, where we could set up for the day. Bert stood next to me and shook his head slowly from side to side.

"This is rubbish, it's packed. Let's try further down."

This was not up for discussion as he immediately turned and started to walk along the seafront, I followed. I kept looking over at intervals, searching for gaps amongst the picnicking families and lobster-red sunbathers, but Bert just kept on moving ahead.

"How far are we going?" I asked him.

"I know a place where it will be much less busy," he answered, he offered me a sherbet lemon from the paper bag in his hand and carried on.

We arrived at the part of the beach near the stone shed that houses the lifeboat. The best thing about that is that you can go in for free and look around at all the old photos, models and life jackets. If you have a spare coin, you can put it in the top of a miniature lifeboat station, and a tiny boat pops out and slides down a ramp. Across the road is where the sand dunes start, there were indeed far fewer people here. Bert seemed satisfied, climbing over the low wall and walking onto the beach.

"This is no good," I told him, "We can't swim here." I pointed at the red flag hanging limply at the top of its pole. Bert smiled at me.

"That's just for the grockles," he told me, "we'll be all right, we live here."

I didn't fully understand the logic of Bert's argument, but I couldn't find any fault in his reasoning – it was true that all the signs and posters around town and on the seafront were there for the holidaymakers, and we were definitely not tourists. We found a nice large area of sand, where we put our stuff down to claim it for ourselves before we started to change into our trunks under our towels.

I have to admit that I had some reservations when we got to the water's edge. The reason for the flags on this part of the beach is that the sandbar is closer to the shore, meaning the tidal current runs much faster here than on any other part of the beach, it also gets much deeper much sooner. I stood and looked at the swirling eddies and currents rushing past me and wondered if this was a good idea after all.

Bert appeared to have no such misgivings, with a laugh and a shout, he plunged forward into the water with an exuberant splash. I watched as he was swept into the water and away from me before he surfaced and started to swim back to the beach. He emerged onto the sand about twenty yards further down, laughing and shaking a shower of glistening water droplets from his hair.

"Your turn," he shouted to me and pointed at the water.

I didn't want Bert to think I was a coward, although inwardly, I knew that I was. The water looked cool and inviting now, and the sun was starting to gather strength for the coming day. I took a deep breath, braced myself and stepped forward. It was cold. I had thought it would be warm, what with the sun beating fiercely down on us, but I was wrong. The frigid water took my breath away, and the swirling current whisked my legs out from underneath me. As I plunged under the water, my open mouth gulped in a generous swig of brine. I coughed and spluttered it out when my head finally emerged back into the air. I was disorientated and panicking slightly as I couldn't see the shore anymore, only to find that when I looked behind me, it was still there. I rushed past Bert, who was laughing so hard he had to bend and put his hands on his knees.

Finally, my survival instincts kicked in, and I started to kick my way gracelessly towards the beach. By the time I made it ashore, I was some way from my starting point. Bert had run after me and was waiting on the sand, watching me as I came ashore.

"How great was that?" he asked, "You went miles."

I lay on my back, breathless, feeling the sand sticking to my wet body, and looked up at Bert. He was doing what I assumed was an impression of me floundering about in the sea, spitting water and trying to swim. For a moment, I wanted to be cross; I'd nearly drowned after all. Then, looking at the comical expression on Bert's face, I burst out laughing.

"C'mon, let's do it again," he suggested. Despite the scare I had last time, I agreed. We ran back up the beach to our starting point and threw ourselves in again. This time, I was prepared, I did not get disorientated or drink anything and found myself enjoying the experience of being pulled along the beach as I made my way back to safety. Bert was beside me, and together, we clambered onto the sand and ran back up for another go.

Time passed quickly as we went back and forth, making up different rules for each new game; you have to swim out two strokes before you start coming back, you have to go completely under the water at least once, we have to start together and see how far one of us can get without using their arms and legs. There were endless variations in this simple game. We carried on until we both agreed that we were tired and went and sat on our towels, drying off quickly in the heat of the sun.

I was pushing the sand around into piles with my feet, and Bert was filtering out small stones that he then proceeded to throw into the water. The sea and the sky blurred together on the horizon, and a hopeful seagull landed in front of us, strutting around in case we might be a good food source. Bert threw a stone in its direction, but it hopped effortlessly out of the way and continued to patrol the sand. Bert looked at me.

"It's an albatross, for fuck's sake!"

We both erupted into laughter. I had a taped copy of 'Monty Python Live at Drury Lane' at home in my bedroom. I would listen to it surreptitiously when my parents weren't around. My dad didn't approve, even though he watched the show when it was on TV. Like many boys my age, I knew every word by heart. Together, we began to recite the sketch where John Cleese tries to sell an albatross to audience members. We moved swiftly on to some of the other sketches, laughing at ourselves as we repeated the memorised words. The Parrot Sketch, the four Yorkshiremen, argument, we knew them all.

The hilarity culminated with us giving a tuneless rendition of the Lumberjack song. As we reached the halfway point of the song, laughing to ourselves at the seemingly ludicrous notion of a man wearing women's clothes, a voice spoke behind us, "What are you then? Fairies?"

We stopped abruptly and turned around to find Alan and Tubs looming over us. Alan was tall and skinny with long dark hair and a permanent scowl, an unfriendly-looking version of his younger brother. Tubs was wearing the same grubby shirt he had been wearing in the park the other day when he had taken my bike.

"Piss off, Al!" Bert snapped.

In a flurry, Alan threw the denim jacket that he had been carrying over his shoulder onto the sand and dropped heavily on top of Bert, holding him in a headlock.

"What did you say, Robert?" he rubbed the top of Bert's head with his knuckles, "Hmm, want to say it again?"

"I said, piss off, leave us alone, you wanker."

The last words were muffled as Alan pushed Bert's head down into the sand, Tubs stood behind us, laughing and egging Alan on.

"Don't let the little squirt talk to you like that, punch him."

I was paralysed, there was nothing I could think of to do or say that would make any difference to what was happening. I tried to stand up, but as soon as I did, Tubs stepped forward and pushed my chest, knocking me back onto the sand.

"Keep out of it unless you want some of this," he held his bunched fist in front of himself, and I decided I didn't want any of that. Bert was squirming underneath his brother, ineffectually trying to hit out while swearing with every other word. Alan was holding him down with no apparent effort, using his weight to keep Bert on the sand. Just as I was wondering what was going to happen next and if I should try getting up again, Alan stood up, leaving Bert lying at his feet with lines of sand stuck to his face where he had been crying.

"You two pansies better stay out of our way, or there'll be worse than that."

"Bugger off, I'm telling Mum when I get home."

Alan was suddenly on him again, pulling the back of his trunks up as high as he could, making Bert stand up on his tip toes as the fabric was pulled up into his scrotum. The look on his face confirmed that it was painful.

"No, you won't, not if you know what's good for you."

He let go, leaving Bert to drop to his knees, cupping his balls in his hands and crying again.

"I'll see you later," grinned Alan, "c'mon, Tubs, let's not hang around here, you don't know where they've been. Let's go and see who's at the amusements."

"Alright," Tubs replied, "hang on, though." He stepped over to us, and before I even realised what he was going to do, he picked up my plimsolls, I made to grab them back, but he held them up over his head and grinned at me. "Do you want them? Do you? Well, go and get them then." He threw them towards the sea. One landed on the edge of the shore, the other splashed into the water and started to wash down the beach with the current. I started to run after it, eventually catching up with it and fishing it out.

By the time I got back, Alan and Tubs were gone, and Bert was changing into his clothes.

"You ok?" I asked.

"Yeah, did you get your shoe back?"

"Yeah," I held up the dripping plimsoll as proof.

"Sorry about that, he's a bloody bastard."

I didn't really know what to say. It seemed like poor form to say bad things about someone else's brother.

"That Tubs is a fucker too," I offered.

Bert made a peculiar face, he stopped pulling his shirt over his bright pink shoulders and looked directly at me.

"He's even worse than Alan, I hate him."

I didn't ask why, having met him twice so far this summer, I was inclined to agree. Bert was now almost fully dressed, so I had to hurry to catch up. It was evident that our trip to the beach was finished for the day. I wrapped my towel around myself and pulled off my trunks. I was covered in sand, which I did my best to remove before putting my clothes back on. It smarted when I tried to wipe my neck, and I realised that my own back must be as red as Bert's.

The attempt to brush myself down made little difference; I still had grains on every part of me and in every crevice.

Bert waited as I finished up, he had produced a comb from somewhere that he was using to scrape the tangles out of his long dark hair, pulling the fringe down over his face, then carefully parting it in the middle and flicking it back. I ran my fingers over my scalp, light brown and cut short enough to ensure that it constantly stuck out in a variety of conflicting angles – Mum wouldn't let me grow it long because it would be 'too much faff' - then we were ready. My wet shoe squelched as we started the long, hot walk home through the alleys and shortcuts that we both knew so well.

As we reached the end of Bert's road, he showed no sign of turning down it. He didn't even slow down.

"Aren't you going home?"

"Nah, I'll wait for Mum to get back from work before I go back."

"Do you want to come round mine?"

"Nah, it's okay. I'll just go for a walk in the park; she'll be back soon, I expect."

Neither of us had a watch on, so we had no real idea of what the time was. Our best guess, based on the fact that the sun was starting to feel a bit less hot and we were both hungry, was that it would soon be teatime.

"Alright, see you tomorrow then?" I asked

"Yeah, see ya. That was fun today until those bastards ruined it."

"Yeah, bastards."

I waved over my shoulder as I turned towards the row of semi-detached houses that my own home sat in the middle of. I didn't turn and look back; I just went to my door and let myself in with the key from the flowerpot. If I had turned back, maybe I would have seen Bert standing, wondering what to do next, or crossing over to the bench at the bus stop and sitting himself down. Maybe even doing what he had said he would and taking himself for a walk.

Despite Bert's assertions that nobody would know if I'd been swimming in the sea, they did. Mum hit the roof when she got back from work, calling me downstairs to the kitchen where she stood holding up the wet and sandy swimming gear that I had left by the washing machine. It was twice as bad because the towel I had used was, apparently, a 'good bath towel', which was the first time I had been made aware of the fact that there was a hierarchy of towels in our house. I assured her that I had only been swimming on the main bit of the beach, where there were lots of people around, and that I had not gone out of my depth.

Mum still went on a bit about Kevin Freeman, who had drowned last summer. It had been a big deal at the time; he had been at the beach with his family. Everyone was having a good day until his parents realised Kevin was no longer with them. They had scoured the busy beach shouting his name, only stopping when they heard a scream from further along the shore, where Kevin's body had bobbed to the surface.

After that, notices appeared along the seafront, alerting people to the dangers of swimming in the sea. They also gave dire warnings about not letting children swim alone. For a while, kids were intensively supervised by concerned parents, even though I was a good swimmer, I was confined to splashing about in the shallows by the beach while Dad stood waist-deep in the water to ensure that I didn't get dragged under or swept out to sea.

I didn't know Kevin; he was a couple of years younger than me, so probably not as good a swimmer as I am. I listened to Mum attentively until I was sent upstairs, which is where I had been anyway, and told to 'wait 'till your father gets home'. I knew this would be late again and that he would be exhausted when he got back, so I wasn't too worried. I lay on my bed and listened to the Crimp twins playing in the street. They had some rolled-up sheets of newspaper that they were using as swords, seeing who could hit the other the hardest with their makeshift weapons. Mostly, it involved shouting at each other until one of them fell, then it involved crying and running indoors to find their mum.

I put on my Monty Python tape, but it didn't seem that funny anymore today. Instead, I listened to Showaddywaddy; I had been keen on this since Gran got it for me last year and had played it so often that it was beginning to wear out, having got tangled up a couple of times. I was starting to realise how limited my selection of home-taped music was. I figured I might see if Bert had anything different that I could borrow to make a copy of tomorrow. I made a mental note to ask him when I next saw him.

FOUR

Bert didn't show up after I had finished tidying the kitchen. I walked Max to the paper shop to get Mum's Woman's Own magazine, cleverly managing to combine the last two jobs on today's list. I'm not sure why Mum gets this every week. I've tried reading it, and it's boring. Also, she doesn't need to know forty-one different ways to do her hair because she always has it the same. The deal was sweetened considerably by the fact that she left enough money for me to get the Beano as well. I didn't get that in the end. I dithered but eventually decided that she wouldn't mind if I got Look In instead – it did have a picture of The New Avengers on the cover, so I thought it would be okay, even though it cost a bit more.

I lay in my room and flicked through my new magazine, realising how much great stuff I was missing on the telly, before deciding that if Bert wasn't coming, then maybe I should go round and call for him. I would have rung him, but our phone has a little lock on the dial to stop us (meaning me) from making unnecessary and expensive phone calls. I was still in the middle of a sporadic hunt for where the key had been hidden since the last time I found it. I thought maybe I wouldn't take my swimming costume today, not after yesterday, I would wait a couple of days for Mum to forget that. Plus, my shoulders were still quite sore and red.

Bert answered his door after two rings of the bell. He looked around the frame, and I could see that he had a dark bruise on the side of his eye.

"Wow! That's a shiner," I blurted.

"Yeah, Al thumped me after I told Mum what he did," his face broke into a smile, "right in front of Mum too. He's in so much trouble, he had to go to Dad's today so he wouldn't pick on me again. He was so pissed off, Dad's strict. Serves him right, eh?"

Bert's Dad doesn't live with them. He has a house on the other side of town. I don't know that much about him; Bert rarely mentions him, and if he does, it's not usually very polite. Bert threw the door open and gestured for me to come in.

"We've got the house to ourselves. I'm not supposed to go out until my eye looks a bit better, so we'll have to hang around here."

I didn't mind, I liked Bert's house, it had a telly for a start. It was already on in the corner of the sitting room, and I was drawn to it like a moth to a flame, standing in the middle of the floor as Belle and Sebastion got up to something or other. I didn't know what, as I had missed the start. I almost protested when Bert walked over and switched it off; the screen dwindled to a small white dot before vanishing completely.

"Do you want to listen to Holy Grail?" he asked.

Of course I did, Monty Python and The Holy Grail had come out last year. It had only been at the cinema for a short time, and it had been an absolute no from Dad when I had asked if he would take me. The soundtrack would do for now; I practically ran up the stairs after Bert.

It wasn't long before we were in Bert's bedroom, cluttered with comics and toys. We were sitting under a poster of the Glitter Band (not so good without Gary, but ok), roaring with laughter. Bert had heard it before, of course, he kept hitting the rewind button to hear his favourite bits again, and I knew the catchphrases were going to be incorporated as a part of our interactions from now on. I asked if he could make me a copy if I gave him a tape. When he said it wasn't a problem, I was reminded that I had intended to ask what else he had that I could make a copy of to augment my meagre music collection.

With a devilish grin, he led me out of the door and into the adjoining room, Alan's bedroom. It was dark and gloomy in here; the curtains were closed, and bare amounts of sun showed the piles of discarded clothes and an unmade bed. It smelt of aftershave and body odour in equal measure, and possibly cigarette smoke – although I couldn't be certain about that.

A disorganised pile of record covers and sleeves had been left lying near a music centre, which had a record player and a built-in tape player set in the same unit.

"Wow, cool," I stepped forward for a better look at it, "that must've cost a bomb."

"Dad got it for him. He buys albums, then records them to sell to his mates. He gets his money back and makes a profit."

"How much does he sell them for?"

"I don't know, he rips people off. We can do it for free when he's not here."

"Won't he mind?"

"He'd go apeshit, I'm not even supposed to come into his room, let alone touch his stuff," as he said this, Bert moved past me and switched on the music centre. It made a low buzzing sound as the small windows lit up, showing rows of tiny numbers and small needles, like miniature versions of the speedometer in my dad's car. He pushed some of the records around with his foot and muttered to himself, "What shall we listen to first?" With that, he picked up a sleeve with no writing, just a black background and a triangle with a rainbow coming out of it.

"What's that?"

"Just listen, you'll see."

I listened, and I saw – or rather, I heard. This was not like anything I had ever come across before. It was big, it filled the room, it was weird. I liked it; it definitely wasn't Rod Stewart or Simon and Garfunkel. We listened for a bit, and then Bert swapped it for a Queen LP, which neither of us was as keen on. After a few tracks, we swapped it for a David Bowie record from a few years ago. I'd heard some of his songs on the radio and found myself liking this even though I didn't get who Ziggy Stardust was, it didn't completely make sense at the time.

"Can I get a tape of this one?"

"Yeah, bring around a blank, and I'll do it for you."

Bert touched the side of his face,

"Does it hurt?" I asked.

"Not really, do you think it's less black now?"

I didn't really, but I sensed that Bert wanted the answer to be yes, so I told him it did.

"Good, that means we can go out."

He was out of the room before I had even got off the bed, I hurried to follow him downstairs, where he had stopped to put his shoes on. I started to walk towards the front door, but Bert went in the other direction,

"This way, Shorts, I'll show you something. It's really good."

We went into his back garden and walked to the back fence, where Bert bent down and lifted a loose bit of panelling.

"Through here, you might have to squeeze a bit."

I did have to wriggle through, followed by Bert, who stood beside me as I took in the scene. We were behind one of the railway arches at the back of the garage that occupied the curved expanse of stained red brickwork. There was a dented, rusting car sitting in the middle of the space, or at least what was left of a car. All the glass, chrome and rubber had been removed, and blocks of wood took the place of one of the wheels. Once, it had been blue, with double headlights and fins at the back. The seats (which were still intact, if a bit dusty and dirty) were leather, and both front and back stretched the entire width of the car.

Surrounding this were piles of old car parts, bits of engines, metal drums and unidentifiable objects that had some connection to the automobile industry, although I had no idea what that might be. The dominant feature of the whole yard appeared to be rust and grease.

The ground was packed with dark earth with patches where things had leaked in pools, staining it black and making everything smell of oil.

"Are we supposed to be here?" I asked.

"No, but it's okay if nobody catches us," Bert answered as he walked over and pulled the car door open with a creak before sitting in the driver's seat of the car. I walked around and joined him on the passenger side, which had no door. We sat pressing switches, moving the gearstick and pretending to steer the car for a while.

"Do you want to see something cool?" Bert asked. He didn't wait for me to answer, he was out of the car and navigating his way across the yard towards the arch. I caught up with him as he was pulling what looked like a tarnished plate from a pile of detritus, he held a finger to his lips and walked to a large green tank near the closed door that led out from the workshop. I watched as he turned the spigot, and some drops of fluid splashed into the shallow container that I now recognised as a hub cap. He started to carry it carefully to the back of the yard, with me in tow.

"What is it?" I asked once we were a safe distance from the door.

"I'll show you," he said as we reached an out-of-sight nook near the rear of the space, penned in by piles of old tyres. He placed the hubcap on the floor without spilling any of the liquid before he started to dig around in his pocket.

"Here," he said, holding up a box of matches.

"Where did you get them?"

"Al's room, just now, watch this."

He took a match from the box, struck it and dropped it into the liquid. As soon as it hit the surface, it became a pool of flickering flames, licking around the rim and fluttering like a silent flag. But my eye was drawn to Bert's hand; blue and yellow flames flickered from his fingertips in the places that they had been splashed as he ferried his cargo, he waved his hand, which only seemed to intensify the flames. Before I even had time to be properly scared, he promptly sat down with his hand firmly underneath him. I half expected the flames to spread to his jeans and start burning their way up his body, but they didn't. Instead, he pulled his hand out and looked at his unblemished fingers.

"Shit, that was close," he laughed, and I laughed with him, relieved that he was okay. We sat down on a couple of tyres and turned our attention back to the hub cap, watching, mesmerised by the dancing flames. Bert reached back into his pocket and pulled out a slightly crumpled cigarette, which he held up and showed me.

"I got this from Al's room, too, wanna try it?"

"He'll kill you if he finds out."

Bert shrugged,

"Well, I'm not going to tell him."

He put the end of the cigarette in his mouth and picked up the matchbox again. He struck one, held it to the tip of the cigarette and breathed in. As quickly as he had done this, he breathed out again, blowing out a mouthful of smoke and coughing as he did so. He then tentatively lifted his hand and tried again, this time not coughing quite as badly. He held it out to me,

"Want some?"

"You made it look tempting," I said sarcastically. But I was tempted, I nearly reached out to take it from him. It was only the thought of the trouble I'd be in with Mum if she found out that stopped me. Bert took a couple more puffs, had a couple more coughs, then tossed the half-smoked cigarette into the now flagging flames as our bonfire burned itself merrily away into oblivion.

"Have you done that before?" I asked, pointing at the hub cap.

"The smoking?"

"No, the fire thing."

"No, but it's only paraffin. I saw Al and his friends do it when they were supposed to be looking after me once. Did you see what was by the garage door?"

I admitted that I hadn't.

"Bottles," Bert told me, "a whole bunch of them. If we sneak back and get them, we can get the deposits."

"What if they catch us?"

"We'll run away, come on – but be quiet."

In the end, we didn't need to try that hard to be quiet, some machine or other started up with a series of clanks and a loud grinding sound inside the workshop. It was so noisy they wouldn't have heard a marching band. We helped ourselves to several empty Corona bottles each, pushing them ahead of ourselves before we wormed our way back through the fence into Bert's garden. We carried the big glass bottles with their dimpled tops through the house to the street, from where we took our prizes to the shop to exchange them for some sweets.

Bert got some Spangles while I opted for the luxury of a quarter of bull's eyes. We were sharing our booty as we took the return journey back to his house. The sun was shining again, the pavements were empty, and we were riding on a sugar high as we turned into Bert's road. Looming in front of us, blocking the pavement, was Tubs.

He was wearing the same grubby shirt as the last two times I had seen him and a pair of flares that draped, frayed and ripped on the pavement.

"Hello, girls," he grinned, "Where's Al?" He addressed the last directly to Bert, who answered,

"He's at his dad's house."

"Alright, what are you two doing?"

"Nothing," replied Bert.

"Are they sweets?" he was addressing me now, I stuttered an answer,

"Yeah, bull's eyes."

"Nice, can I have one?"

I tentatively held the open bag out in my hand. Tubs leaned over as if to look in and select one. Then, with no warning, he spat into the bag.

"Oops, silly me," he laughed to himself, "I guess you won't want them now, will you?"

He guessed right, and I wordlessly let him take the bag from me. Bert was not as quiet,

"You bastard," he shouted.

Tubs immediately pulled himself up to his full height and stepped towards Bert, towering over him.

"What did you call me?"

"A bastard."

I was starting to back nervously away, awed by Bert's bravery but scared for both his and my safety. Tubs seemed momentarily taken aback by Bert's defiance, he took a small step backwards, then leaned in again and grabbed the front of Bert's tee shirt and snarled, "You better look out, I'm going to get you, you little poofter."

Then he let go, giving Bert a shove backwards at the same time. Before he had regained his balance, Tubs had pushed past and was dipping into the bag of sweets and chuckling to himself as he walked away.

"He's the one who needs to watch out, I'll bloody get him," Bert said to me. He was red in the face, and his fists were balled at his sides. I tried to pacify him.

"It's okay, we'd eaten half of them already," I said.

"I don't care. I'll get him one day, you'll see."

I was quietly dubious; Tubs was quite a lot bigger than either of us, and I'd heard that he had a reputation for fighting. I decided not to say anything, keeping step alongside Bert as he continued back towards home. Suddenly, he turned to me and smiled.

"It's okay anyway, we've still got these," he held up his two packets of Spangles and then passed one of them to me. "Do you want to come and watch telly?"

Of course, I didn't need to be asked twice about that. We went back and made ourselves comfortable on the sofa until Bert's mum got back. Taking this as my cue to leave, I gathered up my pile of empty sweet wrappers and dragged myself reluctantly away from 'Go With Noakes' and his adventures with the red arrows. On the short walk home, I imagined myself flying in a jet plane, soaring along the straights and banking around the corners until I finally came in to land through the front door.

FIVE

"I'm back, sorry I'm late," I pushed the front door closed behind me with my foot. Only half of that was true, but I didn't want to be in trouble again. "What's for tea?"

To my surprise, it wasn't Mum but Auntie Jean who came out of the kitchen, I could see Mum sitting at the table behind her with her back towards me.

"Hello, love, did you have a good day?"

I was a bit taken aback. Usually, nobody asked me that. It was more like 'Where have you been?' and 'Did you stay out of trouble?'

"Yes, I went round Bert's." I decided Auntie Jean probably wouldn't want to know about the setting fire to things or stealing the garage's empty bottles. She definitely wouldn't want to know about me getting picked on by Tubs.

"That's nice, dear, I'm glad you had fun."

I like Auntie Jean; she only says nice stuff, and she doesn't mind what I've been up to. I decide to risk asking her about tea.

"Oh, my goodness, you must be hungry," she answered, "I didn't realise the time. Here, let me see what I can do." She took her purse out of her handbag and dug around for some coins, then passed me two ten-pence pieces and a five, "Get yourself some fish and chips, love, me and your mum are…well, we're busy."

I didn't ask what they were busy doing, despite her pleasant manner, Auntie Jean had looked serious when I came in. That, and the fact that Mum hadn't shouted at me to take my shoes off, made it clear that whatever they were busy doing, it was none of my business. I said thank you for the money, put it carefully into my pocket, and then disappeared back out of the door.

I could have got fish and chips, but sausages were cheaper. I guessed that Auntie Jean wasn't going to know or ask for her change, which would mean that I would have some money left over for tomorrow. I collected my meal and went to sit on the bench at the bus stop, balancing the newspaper carefully on my lap and savouring the smell of the vinegar before unwrapping it and consuming my feast.

As I finished my last few chips and wiped my greasy fingers on the paper, I was joined on the bench by two boys who were also having an al fresco tea. A short kid called Glen whose mum is a teacher at our school, worst luck for him, I guess. The other kid was wearing glasses held together with tape; I couldn't remember his name, it might have been Mike, or Michael, or Mickey. Or maybe Dave. They are both in my year at school. They're not in any of my classes, but I know both of them well enough to say hi to them. After we had ascertained that we were all 'alright', I got up to put my chip paper in the bin. Just as I started to walk away from the bench, Glasses asked, "Hey, Shorts, your dad's a fireman, isn't he?"

"Yeah," I replied. I stopped and turned back to face them, wondering why he would ask that.

"He's not one of the ones that's missing, is he?"

"What ones that are missing?"

"It was on the news," said Glen, "some firemen got cut off on the moors, everyone's looking for them."

"What, on Dartmoor?"

"Duh, yeah. The wind changed, and they got stuck on the wrong side of the fire."

I was hit with the dawning realisation that everything at home had not been how it was supposed to be. I had been so distracted by the offer of fish and chips that it hadn't occurred to me that there was a reason for Auntie Jean to be around. Or a reason for Mum not coming to tell me off for the state I was in. There was a weird feeling in my stomach, maybe a bit sick – maybe a bit scared. It wouldn't be my dad, though, he knew what he was doing, he'd been a fireman for years. He would probably be at home right now.

"No, I don't think so, he's probably back from work now," I answered, trying to sound more certain than I felt.

Glen and Glasses watched me throw my chip paper towards the bin. It missed, but I just left it on the ground and started to run towards home. As I turned into the road, I could feel my heart starting to pound. Then I saw a police car parked directly outside our house, with the Crimp twins standing on their tiptoes to peer into its windows. Oblivious of anything but my mission to get home and see Dad, I sprinted at full tilt.

I burst through the door just as a policeman was about to come out. He quickly stepped aside.

"Alright, lad? Slow down, or you'll hurt yourself."

I ignored him and went directly to the kitchen, where Mum was standing by the sink with her eyes all red and her coat in her hand. When she saw me, she dropped the coat and wrapped her arms around me, pulling me into her breast. I was almost too surprised to speak, she never usually did that, so now I knew for certain that something was wrong.

"Mum, where's Dad?" I asked as I managed to pull back a little, "Is he okay?"

"They're not sure. I'm sorry I should have told you earlier. Everybody's out looking for him, and you mustn't worry."

"But you're worried." It occurred to me, for the first time, that Dad's job was not just about racing around in the fire engine with the blue lights flashing and the sirens on. Maybe it could be a dangerous job, too.

Mum looked around for support, and Auntie Jean stepped in.

"We're sure everybody is doing everything they can and that your dad is safe and sound. Your mum was just a bit surprised, that's all. They think they know where your dad is; they just can't get to him at the moment, but him and Bill will be keeping themselves safe."

Bill is my dad's fireman friend who comes around ours to help Dad with stuff and drink beer sometimes. I like Bill, he's funny and a bit rude – which makes Mum tell him off. Not like she tells me off, though, it's more kind of jokey. If it's Dad and Bill, I'm pretty sure they'll be okay, they can do anything. Still, I am a little bit worried.

"I'm going with the policeman to wait and see him when they get back to the station. I want you to stay with Auntie Jean – and be good!"

I was hopeful for a moment that she meant I should go to Auntie Jean's house with her – which would mean getting to watch some telly. Sadly, that was not the plan. Mum went off in the police car with all the neighbours watching. Auntie Jean settled down in the kitchen with her knitting, which she had pulled out of her bag like the magicians on telly make rabbits appear from hats. I went upstairs to read the rest of my Look-In. I wasn't taking it in, though. My bedroom door opened, and Auntie Jean came in with a mug of steaming hot chocolate. She'd made it with milk, too, a rare luxury in our house. She sat on the bed beside me and put her arm across my shoulders. I could smell her perfume, flowery and sweet, and was glad she had come to talk to me.

"I'm sure your dad will be fine, you need to get to bed now, you'll feel better for some sleep. Are you okay?"

I assured her I was and took a slurp of the chocolate. I thought it would be weird to have a hot drink on such a warm evening, but it was okay – nice, in fact. I also thought I wouldn't be able to get to sleep, but I was soon dead to the world under the single sheet that was all I needed that summer. My new lucky penny was tucked safely under the pillow, still warm from where I had been clutching it in my hand, leaving a semi-circular imprint in my palm.

At some point in the night, I half-woke, hearing whispering voices from downstairs. The front door was quietly opened and closed, and someone was making a drink in the kitchen. I dozed back off, only dimly registering the sound of my bedroom door being stealthily opened and then shut again before the house went quiet once more.

The next morning, I went into Mum and Dad's bedroom as soon as I woke up. Mum was there on her own, awake but still in bed.

"Did they find him?" I asked.

"Yes, dear, yes they did." The look of relief on her face as she told me this was enough to let me know that he was okay.

"Where is he? Did he have to go back to work?"

Mum was sitting up by now in her flowery nightie,

"No, he's in the hospital…"

"The hospital?"

"Yes, the hospital. He's fine they just wanted to keep an eye on him and Bill tonight to make sure they were both okay, he'll be coming home later. He's going to be at home for the next few days, so you'll need to be on extra good behaviour."

"I will, I promise."

"Good, you can make me a coffee while I get dressed, then put your clothes on and take Max for a walk, please."

I hurried to do the things I had been asked, then spent the rest of the morning waiting impatiently for Dad to get back. I did all the helpful things I could think of, like making my bed, putting the magazines straight on the coffee table and asking regularly when Dad would be back. Mum had taken the lock off the phone and spent most of her time sitting by the front door, busily reassuring everybody who rang that Dad was fine. She rang Grandma and let her know what had happened, which was the longest of her calls. But mostly, she waited to find out when Dad would be leaving the hospital.

It was from listening to these phone calls from the top of the stairs that I got the gist of what had happened yesterday. Dad and Bill had been putting out a patch of gorse fire. They had moved slightly away from the other firefighters when a gust of wind had blown across the area that they had just beaten, bringing the flames back to life. They were never in any real danger; they just couldn't get back to the safety of the fire engine and had to walk around a long circular route to get back to the rest of the crew, by which time the light had started to fade, and the alarm had been raised.

I didn't think this would be too bad for Dad as he liked walking on the moors anyway, I'm not sure about Bill. By chance, there had been a TV camera crew on the moors at the time. They didn't miss the opportunity to report the story as it happened, adding a bit of excitement to their regular updates about the fires that had been a feature of the summer so far. I was given some money to go down and get the newspaper, as someone had phoned Mum to tell her that the story was in one of them – along with pictures of Dad and Bill.

I read the article in the paper on my way back. It didn't tell me anything new, but it did say that Dad and Bill were 'brave heroes', which made me feel quite proud. When I arrived back with the paper, there was a strange car outside the house, a blue Ford Cortina that the twins were busy inspecting. I rushed inside, and there was Dad at our table. He got up and swept me into his arms, giving me the biggest hug, then started coughing and put me down again.

"There," said Mum, "now you've overdone it. You need to go and lie down."

"I'm fine, give me a moment." He sat back down and talked to me, he still smelt of bonfires, perhaps even more than he usually did, although that could have been my imagination.

"Are you okay?"

"I'm fine, you're in the paper. They said you were a brave hero."

"Well, I'm not so sure about that, but I'm sorry if I gave you all a scare." He looked up at Mum when he said this, and she smiled back at him. Then he started coughing again, and mum chivvied him upstairs to lie down while I made him a cup of tea. When I took it into him, he grinned and told me it looked great, better than the ones the pretty nurses had bought him in the hospital. Then he laughed, which made him start to cough again.

Mum gave him a look and told him it served him right, then led me out of the room, closing the door behind us.

"Dad's going to have to rest for a day or two, which means he's going to need some peace and quiet. Do you think you can manage that?"

I thought I could, but I was quite pleased when Mum suggested that maybe I should go and see if my friend wanted to play so Dad could have a sleep.

SIX

Bert answered the door.

"Shit, I saw your dad on the news, is he still at the hospital?"

"No, he's home now. Was he really on the news?"

"Yeah, they had a picture of him and the other fireman."

"Cool, it was in the paper too."

I was a bit disappointed that I had missed seeing Dad and Bill on the telly, maybe we would get one again now – so we don't miss him if he's on again. Bert shouted back into the house that he was going out, then joined me outside without waiting for an answer.

"Alan's back, he's mad because he thinks I went in his room yesterday."

"You did."

"I know, but he can't prove it, and he had the riot act read to him by Mum and Dad. He has to leave me alone."

I didn't know what the riot act was, but I guessed it meant Alan got told off. It served him right. We started walking away from the house towards the park while Bert fired questions at me about Dad, and I answered as best I could, given that I didn't know any more than anybody else. We didn't make a conscious decision to go to the park, it was just the closest place to aim for. It was nearby, at the end of the road, in fact. There would be some shade to sit in, so it was okay by me. We went through the gates, across the grass, and then scrambled up into the lowest branches of the giant Oak tree that dominated the central space.

Sitting in the shade on one of the broad lower branches, we could see most of the park, the kiddie's area teeming with small children, with benches full of women sitting and talking. The pond with its layer of bright green algae glistening in the sun. We had a good view of the sloped path where some kids had a homemade go-kart that they were taking turns to steer down towards the road and the two bottom gates that led in and out of the park.

"So, do you think you'll be a fireman when you grow up?" Bert asked.

"Dunno seems okay; Dad gets to see his mates and ride in the fire engine every day. What about you?"

"Might do, or I might join the army and get trained for special missions. Then I can come back and duff up Al."

He laughed and then spat. I tried to spit even further and failed. We repeated this a couple of times, with Bert being the clear winner each time. The competition ended when I managed to dribble all down the front of my shirt in a poorly judged attempt to change the speed and trajectory of my next effort.

"Do you want to go higher up the tree?"

I didn't, I wasn't keen on getting too high,

"Na, it's too hot for that. We could go and muck about by the pond."

"Yeah, okay, hey, what's that?"

He pointed to the sloping path, where two more boys had arrived to join the go-kart racers. Both of them were carrying short pieces of wood. We watched as they walked confidently to the top of the incline and stopped to have a conversation with each other. It became obvious what they were doing in the next few moments. One boy put his piece of timber down, and we could now see it had some wheels fixed underneath it. He put one foot on the top, steadied himself and then picked up the other foot and started rolling down the hill. He quickly gained momentum, running onto the grass where the path turned, causing him to run forward to avoid falling when his board came to an abrupt halt. He gestured for his friend to do the same and waited for him to join him. His friend was not so lucky and ended up rolling on the grass, they both laughed, then picked up their boards and walked back to the top.

"That looks great," Bert said, more to himself than me, "are they skateboards?"

"I think so," we had heard about them, of course, they were all the rage in America. But this was the first time we had seen people using them here, in our park. The two boys started their wobbly descents again, once more running into the grass at the bend – although they did make it slightly further than their first attempt.

"Let's go and look," Bert said as he dropped off the branch onto the ground.

I followed him, and as I landed, I realised that Bert had stopped. Two girls had been walking under the tree, almost underneath us. One of them had blonde hair and a denim waistcoat, and the other was in a patterned vest top with her brown hair tied up in a ponytail, Bert had nearly landed on top of them.

"Watch what you're doing," said the blonde girl, "you nearly hit us."

The girls were a little older than us, I recognised them from around school. The blonde girl was called Janet. I knew this because she hung out with the boys who were always in trouble. The ones who try to sneak out over the wall and into the field to smoke at breaktimes. They were the kids who always seemed to be standing in the corridors outside classrooms or queueing on the line of chairs outside the headmaster's office – the ones you sat on when you were waiting your turn to go in and be caned. Generally, I tried to avoid them, although Tubs, who would often be on the periphery of that group, had made that impossible now.

"Sorry," Bert replied. His tone of voice didn't indicate that he was particularly sorry, the blonde girl looked as though she was about to yell at him, then stopped abruptly.

"Hey, aren't you Alan's little brother? He is Theresa; he's Alan's brother."

Theresa smiled and acknowledged this,

"Yes, he is, I think he's called Robert."

"I'm called Bert," he replied, "and whatever Al's done, it's nothing to do with me."

Janet looked at Theresa and made an odd face,

"He hasn't done anything – yet." She giggled and then asked, "Is Alan at home?"

"Dunno, I'm not his secretary."

"Ooh, you're cheeky. Do you know where he is then?"

The question became moot almost immediately. While we had been distracted talking to the girls, Alan and Tubs had come into the park and made a beeline towards the skateboarding boys. The go-karters had moved further up the road to find steeper slopes to play on. From where we were standing, it was clear that Al and Tubs were demanding that the skateboarders let them have a turn. The two boys looked reluctant but capitulated in the face of the threat of violence from Tubs, who had raised one of his fists. Janet immediately started to walk towards them, Theresa lingered for a moment.

"You're Shorts, aren't you?" she asked me.

"Yes," I answered. I was curious as to how she knew and why she'd asked.

She raised her eyebrows and then started to follow Janet,

"Nice to meet you, Shorts, see you around."

Me and Bert stayed and watched as first Alan, then Tubs managed to fall from their boards almost before they had started. Tubs picked the board up and threw it onto the grass, but Alan reset his and tried again – with similar results.

"They can't do that for toffee, can they?" Bert looked at me, "shall we get out of here? It'll be safe to go back to the house now he's gone."

I showed Bert the handful of change I had left over from my trip to the chip shop last night,

"Sweet shop first? I owe you some."

"Well, now you're talking. Let's go before they see us."

"Do you think they'll give those boys their boards back?" I remembered my first encounter with Tubs.

"When they're bored, yeah."

They clearly weren't bored yet, they had seen Janet and Theresa and had redoubled their ill-fated attempt to look cool. I guessed Bert was right, that they'd get fed up with it soon. We left the park through the gate furthest from them, just in case.

Back at Bert's, with a bag of sweets each, I remembered something, I fished a cassette tape out of my pocket. It was full of music that I'd taped off the radio, most of the songs missed the beginning and finished with the sound of Tony Blackburn or Noel Edmunds talking over the end of them. I'd stuck some tape over the holes on the top edges so that it could be recorded over.

"Can you do the David Bowie one for me, please?"

"Sure, pass it over."

Bert started making the tape. He found some paper and pens in his room so we could make a cover for it. He got the kitchen scissors to cut the paper to the right size and then passed it to me. I painstakingly copied out the track list, wishing my best writing was just a little bit better than it was, while Bert took control of the recording process on his double tape player. Once everything was finished, we went downstairs to watch TV for a bit.

It felt like we had only just sat down when the front door banged open, and Alan, Tubs, Janet and Theresa came noisily into the house.

"I'll just get some different jeans," Alan told the others.

"You wouldn't have ripped those if you'd stayed on the board," teased Janet.

"Piss off. Tubs, get me a drink of orange, I'm thirsty."

We heard Tubs going into the kitchen, followed by the sound of clinking glasses, cupboards opening and closing and the tap running. We could hear that Janet was in the kitchen talking to him, and I assumed we were going to be undisturbed until the sitting room door opened.

"Hello, we meet again, what are you watching?"

"Nothing," answered Bert, getting up to turn it off.

It was too late, though, Theresa had seen that it was the kid's show Bod. We had put it on while we waited for something better. I braced myself for some teasing, but it never came.

"What's the tape?" she asked, nodding at the cassette in my hand. I showed her. After looking at it, she passed it back and nodded approvingly. "Not bad, I thought it was going to be something awful, like Showaddywaddy or some shit."

I scoffed at the idea that it would have been anything as bad as that, making a mental note to tape over my copy as quickly as I could.

"Have you heard any Lou Reed?"

I looked at her completely blankly.

"Lou Reed, Transformer. If you like David Bowie, you'll like that."

Just then, Alan came in, he scowled at us then said,

"Come on, Theresa, we can go now. You won't have these two annoying you."

She turned to follow Alan, but before she left, she turned back and said,

"I'll make a copy for you for the next time I see you."

Then she was gone, leaving a faint smell of something flowery in the space she had occupied. We sat in silence for a moment until Bert turned the TV back on. We'd missed the end of Bod, and now it was cricket, so we turned it off again. Loud music started to reverberate from upstairs, so we went out into the sun in the back garden. The music was just as loud out there, booming out of the open bedroom window. We sat on the back step and picked stones out of the flowerbeds to throw, tossing them over the fence to see if we could make them clang against the rusted old car sitting in the middle of the yard. Eventually, a gruff voice yelled, *'Pack that in, you bloody kids!'* We packed it in. Bert shouted back, *'Pack that in'* –

mimicking the disembodied voice, then we ran off laughing in the direction of the estuary.

The tunnel where the brook passes under the railway line was cool and dry. The bright sun shone in at either end of the short passage, not quite managing to light up the middle, where we sat on the edge of the brook. The rocks under us were covered in streaks of long, dry weed that was turning to dust. The green stripes covered small stones that we picked out and threw into the shallow water as we waited for the train to arrive.

When it passed over us, the sound reverberated all around, making the concrete shake and enveloping us in a cocoon of sound. It was only a short time, but it felt like forever. We both laughed as we waited for the train to reload with fresh passengers at the station. When we heard it begin its journey, we stood with our palms flat against the concrete, feeling the vibrations run through our arms. I felt it arriving above us just as Bert began to shout, a long, drawn-out howl that was drowned out completely by the noise of the train and its carriages. I joined in, and together, we unleashed the full power of our young lungs – insignificant in the face of the much larger competition passing over our heads, leaving us breathless and laughing.

***

Theresa sat in front of the mirror; she piled her hair up on top of her head and then let it go with a sigh. The weather had been so hot it made her long hair sweaty and uncomfortable, even when it was tied back like it had been today. The heat had made everything unbearable, from the snug jeans to the top that had to be big enough to cover the stupid bra that she had only recently started needing to wear. She knew she would have to start pulling out some of her dresses from the wardrobe soon, then deciding which ones she disliked the least. They all seemed a bit garish and, well, flouncy, she supposed. She had briefly considered borrowing one of her sister's bigger tee shirts this morning but decided against it when she remembered the row it had caused the last time she did that. In fairness, she had spilt coke down the front of it. It certainly wasn't worth the risk of that happening again.

Her day had gone from the promise of uninterrupted lazing about while her mum and dad were at work to being busy. All in the space of one phone call. Janet had rung her, Janet, who she had hardly spoken to for the last term of the school year. Janet, who had started hanging around with Sue and Michelle, a couple of bitchy girls that Theresa didn't get on with. At the time, Janet hadn't seemed to have noticed her absence, but now it was the holiday. Sue lived too far away to meet up, and Michelle had gone away on holiday. Still, Theresa supposed it was good to hear from Janet; they had been friends since primary school, after all.

Janet's advances had not been entirely altruistic, however, which didn't surprise Theresa that much. She had decided, in her single-minded Janet way, that she was going to go out with Alan Card. Alan was in the year above them at school. Usually, mixing with someone from a different year group would be a non-starter. But in the holiday, the unwritten rules, social conventions and politics that govern how kids interact seemed to relax a bit, and Janet had decided that Alan was going to be hers.

Theresa wasn't sure what Janet saw in him, he had long, greasy hair, a poor complexion and was usually in trouble for something or other. Also, he hung out with an unlikable kid called Tubs. It seemed to Theresa that every time she saw them, they were either tormenting someone smaller or breaking something. Nevertheless, she had agreed, in the absence of anything else to do, to go with her and call for Alan - as a bit of moral support. She was ready when the bell rang, and together, they had set off in search of Janet's intended target/victim. Janet had gone all out: lipstick, hair done, bust out (she'd been wearing a bra for most of last year), best clothes – as glamourous as a 13-year-old girl could be. Theresa thought Alan didn't stand a chance in the face of this level of determination.

Walking through the park, they were both surprised when there was a rustle of leaves, and two boys fell out of the tree they were passing. Maybe dropped would have been a better description; it had been a controlled descent, but it had still caught them unawares. The boys had seemed to share their surprise. Clearly, they hadn't expected anyone to be walking under them. Theresa recognised them both instantly, even without their school uniforms. They were in the year below her at school, two of the new kids from last year who were rarely seen without each other. They were as different as chalk and cheese and only ever seemed to be called by their nicknames. Bert, a whip-skinny lad with serious eyes, long, straight dark hair and an almost feline grace. Then Shorts – where did he get that name? – crumpled blonde hair, square shoulders and an air of startled rabbit about him. She wasn't sure how two such different boys could be so attached to one another, but they were.

Janet had immediately recognised Bert as Alan's younger brother and had tried to use the situation to her advantage, trying to ascertain the whereabouts of her intended. It had been an unnecessary line of questioning as Alan and Tubs arrived in the park right on cue. Theresa was led away while the younger boys made off in the opposite direction.

As they walked across the yellow grass, she could see that Alan and Tubs had borrowed - or stolen - some skateboards that some other boys had bought to the park. The two skateboarders looked disgruntled, then pleased when Janet approached Alan and distracted both him and Tubs from what they were doing. Tubs threw the board he had just fallen off towards its owner,

"That's shit that is – you want to get a decent one."

He then joined Alan, who had just abandoned his board in the grass and was talking to Janet. What followed was simultaneously comical and excruciating. Alan and Tubs went into showing off overdrive, pushing each other around, climbing onto the roof of the shelter, breaking branches off trees to hit one another with, shouting insults at far-off dog walkers and swaggering around like the football supporters she had seen on the news earlier in the year. In other words, they behaved like yobs. This was evidently for her and Janet's benefit; it was clearly supposed to impress them. Theresa thought they were ridiculous, but Janet – for some unknowable reason – acted as if it was the coolest thing she had ever seen. She laughed at their antics and egged them on when they moved onto each new, stupid idea.

It was a relief when, after being asked to *'please get off the swings and let the children have a turn'* by a flustered-looking mum with a crying child, Alan finally suggested they go back to his house to get a drink. Once they were at a safe distance, Tubs turned round and shouted to the woman that she was a stupid bitch. Janet laughed at this, and Theresa was relieved that at least they would be out of sight of other people. She tagged along behind as Janet walked as closely as she could to Alan. Tubs, sweaty and red-faced, tried to do the same to her, but she managed to keep her distance.

At Alan's house, she was pleasantly surprised to see Bert and Shorts again. They were in the front room watching kid's TV. She would have liked to sit and watch with them for a bit, but they turned it off when she came in. She saw that Shorts was holding a tape in his hand. She asked what it was, although she was most excited when he tentatively held it towards her, and she found out what it wasn't. It wasn't one of those crap bands like Queen or Led Zeppelin. It wasn't any of the asinine bands that filled the charts, nor was it disco pap – or Shwaddywaddy. It was Bowie she was impressed; she liked Bert and Shorts already, they had good taste. Encouraged by what she assumed was his preferred musical genre, she promised to make a tape of Transformer for Shorts for the next time she saw him. Then she was dragged upstairs to suffer listening to Black Sabbath growling their way through We Sold Our Soul For Rock 'n' Roll. Apart from Paranoid, it all grated with her. She was glad when she was finally able to escape and return home.

She decided that she would make Shorts' tape for him straight away, it would distract her from what had been an awkward afternoon and help her forget about Tubs sitting himself next to her and trying his best to look down her top the entire time they were in Alan's room. She borrowed the LP from her sister's room (this was permitted, even though clothes were off-limits) and started to write out the track list while it played. Just for good measure, she decided to put her favourite Iggy Pop album on the other side of the tape, imagining the look of pleasure on Short's face when he heard it for the first time.

SEVEN

The smell of sausages met me as I walked through the front door, Mum shouted at me from the kitchen to take my shoes off and then go and wash my hands. I did what I was told before going back to the kitchen, where Dad was sitting at the table and Mum was stirring up the Smash in a bowl. I sat down across from Dad and smiled at him. He grinned back at me, and it was the happiest I had seen him for a long time.

"Have you had a good day?" he asked.

"Yeah, me and Bert went to the park."

"That sounds good, did you stay out of trouble?"

I thought about it for a moment, then nodded my head.

"Good, I'm sorry if I gave you a scare yesterday."

I wasn't sure for a moment why I would have been scared, I know he can get cross sometimes, but he's not that scary. Then it twigged, he was talking about the fire, about getting separated from his crew on the moors.

"Nah, I knew you'd be alright."

It was true, my youthful optimism and worldview didn't have any place where Dad would not be an invincible being. A reassuring presence that would always be there. Although, since I started getting taller last year, he doesn't seem to tower quite as much anymore.

"Well, I wish I'd had your confidence, it was a bit worrying for a moment when it started to get dark. But it's alright now, thanks for letting me sleep today." He coughed a bit as he finished speaking, holding his hanky up to his mouth. I was a bit surprised at this chink in his usually infallible facade, the only things I'd ever seen him worry about before were the bills.

"Was it like that film The Towering Inferno?" I asked. I hadn't been allowed to go and see that at the cinema, because I was too young, but I knew what it was about.

"Well, it was on the moors, not in a skyscraper, but me and Bill were quite a lot like Steve McQueen and Paul Newman."

"Ooh, you wish," Mum said as she came over and put the plates of food on the table, then she bent and kissed Dad on the cheek. "Eat up, you need your strength."

She was in an exceptionally good mood, for Mum, I enjoyed us all sitting together to eat for a change. I didn't even complain that it was peas, not beans, with the sausage and mash. I wolfed mine down hungrily, in between tentatively suggesting that we could have seen Dad on the TV if we'd had one and asking if I could put the tent up in the garden and have a sleep out. The answers were 'no' and 'we'll see', but everyone seemed happy, and I didn't get told off for anything.

As I was clearing the table, a familiar noise wafted through the open front window, the slightly wonky sound of Greensleeves coming down our road . I looked hopefully at Mum and Dad, expecting the answer to be the usual no, but Mum surprised me by telling me to find her purse and go and get a block of Raspberry Ripple. I didn't have to be asked twice. I located the purse and ran out into the street in my socks, where I queued up behind the Crimp twins and their mum to get our ice cream.

We shared half and put the rest in the freezer, then Mum said,

"Look at your face, go and give it a wash, then give us some peace."

When I looked in the bathroom mirror, there was a bit of ice cream on my chin from where I'd tried to lick the remnants from my bowl. I wiped it off with the hand towel before retreating into my bedroom to listen to the tape Bert had recorded for me. After a couple of listens, I had decided which were my favourite songs. I liked all of them, but Ziggy Stardust and Starman were best, I was rewinding them over and over, trying to write down the words, when the door opened, and Dad came in.

"Time for bed now, do you need a bedtime story?" he smiled as he said it.

"No, I can read my own books now."

"Alright, good night then. Don't let the bed bugs bite."

He tousled my hair and smiled, and I smiled back, although I was also a bit sad. It was true that I could read my own stories now, but it would have been nice to have Dad sit on the end of the bed and read one of the books from my shelf, with the funny voices he used to make for the different characters. Maybe I'd ask him another day, but for now, I switched off my tape player, put my pyjamas on and got into bed. Even with the windows wide open and no blankets, I thought I'd never get to sleep as I tossed and turned in the humid, still darkness.

I woke with a start in the pitch darkness, covered in sweat and shivering. I wrapped the sheet around me and tried to settle back down, but the dream I'd just had wouldn't leave me alone.

Dad had been trapped on the roof of a burning tower block, with flames curling around his feet. I watched as he leapt off and landed in a patch of bracken that had cushioned his fall, then got up laughing and brushing himself off. Then, from behind the foliage, Theresa had appeared. She was wearing a long flowery dress, and her arms were bare, she looked at me and said,

"I had to phone someone, so I picked on you, hey, that's far out, so you heard him too," then she laughed and ran back into the bushes, and Dad was gone.

I wanted to go into Mum and Dad's room, to get in their bed and curl up warm between them, but I was too big for that now. Also, I could hear them both snoring and didn't want to wake them, so I pulled the sheet up to my chin and waited for sleep to catch up with me again.

EIGHT

Mum was still in a really good mood the next morning; she was singing along to Rod Stewart on the radio in the kitchen when I got up. She didn't have any jobs for me today, apart from walking Max in the park. It was already hot, even this early in the morning. Max didn't seem that interested in running around like he normally does, he just peed on some of the clumps of yellow grass and sniffed around the trees with their dried and curling leaves. The only time he seemed to perk up was when we saw other dogs, and then he would run around them, poking his nose into their behinds and barking excitedly. When we got back, he made straight for his water bowl and half emptied it, then went and laid down in the shade of the shed with his tongue lolling out the side of his mouth.

Mum told me that she and Dad were going into town and asked if I would like to come. I don't know what they were going for, but there was no way I wanted to trudge around the hot, sweaty shops, so I politely declined. Mum smiled,

"I thought you might say that I've got your swimming things ready and made you a sandwich. You can go to the beach if you want, but stay at the clock tower end and…"

"Don't go out of my depth," I finished for her. My old primary school plimsoll bag was on the table, with some sandwiches and crisps nestled alongside my trunks and an old towel. I thanked her, packed it all up and got ready to leave before she changed her mind and made me go with them.

"You have a good day, we'll see you later," she called as I opened the front door.

"Sure thing," I answered, and then I was free again.

I took the short walk to Bert's and asked him if he wanted to come with me, he seemed keen and went inside to collect his swimming gear. On the way, I explained the rules to him about staying at the Clock end and not going out deep. He didn't seem too worried, he just agreed with the terms and conditions and stepped alongside me down all the back roads and shortcuts that took us through the rows of terraced houses and past the station, where we walked along the lane full of garages that led to the beach.

Just before we got there, Bert suggested we cut off and walk around Shelly Road. I couldn't think of any reason not to, the way he suggested was always interesting, with lots to look at, it went past the busy docks. We walked along the middle of the sand-covered road, lined with rows of mismatched houses. Each one seemed to be built a different size and style and painted a different colour from its neighbour, most not even in a straight line with each other. I think they were meant to be holiday houses originally, but people live in them all year round now. I told Bert I thought it would be great to have a house that led straight onto a beach, and he replied that it probably would be, but not in the winter. I hadn't even thought of that, I guess he was right, it must get pretty cold and wet when it's stormy.

We reached the docks and stopped on the bridge, watching some fishermen unloading their boat. Rivers of shiny scales cascaded into barrels on the quayside while gulls wheeled overhead, their squawks competing with the shouted conversation and occasional cussing of the boat crew. The air smelt of salt, sea and diesel – but mostly fish.

"Walter Raleigh used to set sail from here, you know," Bert informed me.

I looked at the tiny entrance and found it hard to believe that a boat big enough to sail thousands of miles would fit through it,

"Really?"

"Yep, that's what they told us in primary school."

I still had my doubts but said nothing as we continued on our way, now nearly at our destination. We walked along the busy pavement, looking over the low wall for a promising space as we went.

The least busy part of this bit of beach was the area furthest from the public toilets and ice cream shop. I knew from experience that it was better not to be near the kiosk because that was where the wasps hung out. But I wasn't about to go and start telling the grockles that, especially as it meant that me and Bert got a prime piece of beach real estate to spread our towels on. We changed as quickly as we could and went straight down to the water's edge, where we plunged into the cold water. We swam directly out past the other people and started swimming and messing about in the deeper water. We were treading water and catching our breath when I asked Bert,

"Do you remember Kevin Freeman?"

"Who?"

"Kevin Freeman, that kid who drowned."

"Oh him, yeah, why?"

"That's why my Mum says we should only swim here – and stay in our depth."

"My mum said he only drowned because his mum and dad weren't watching him properly."

It occurred to me that our parents weren't exactly being attentive to what we were doing right now, I said so as we started to swim back to the beach.

"Well, no, but we're watching out for each other, aren't we?"

"I guess."

We were walking back to our staked place now, sand sticking in clumps to our wet feet.

"Of course we are. I've got your back, and you've got mine. Shit, look at your back."

"Why? What is it?"

"You're peeling."

I looked down at my shoulders and saw that he was right, my skin was sloughing off in wrinkles and curls. It had been itchy and sore last night, so it kind of made sense. I was distracted, but not too much so to take on board the importance of what Bert had said. Whatever else happened this summer, we were in it together – best friends.

We swam a couple more times, dousing ourselves in the cold water each time we got too hot sitting on the beach. We made piles of sand that we carefully decorated with shells and small pebbles, then subsequently bombarded with larger stones. The person who demolished the other person's castle first was the winner, one win for me, two for Bert and several draws. I shared my packed lunch, and we watched the little kids go berserk as if they had never been to a beach before. I don't know, maybe they hadn't.

A bit further down the beach was a rickety wooden jetty. It had large rusted wheels so that it could be moved up and down the beach as the tide went in and out. A boat tied up next to it at regular intervals while a man with a megaphone stood on the top of the cabin and announced the next forthcoming trip. Competing with all the other sounds of the busy seaside, he loudly exhorted people to come for a trip around the bay. *'Trips around the bay, all around the bay, for only 20 pence. Children half price, the next trip leaves in ten minutes, you pay on the boat.'* The small blue vessel would fill with a line of happy tourists, all eager to try out their sea legs. It then dropped its mooring line and chugged off up the coast, returning half an hour later to start all over again.

All morning, the tide had been going out, and the jetty had to be regularly moved further down the beach to make sure the water was deep enough for the boat to dock. But in the afternoon, not long after the sandwiches were gone, the tide changed. Now, the jetty had to be pulled back again to stop it from being submerged. Bert had been watching it carefully. Suddenly, he jumped up,

"Come on, shorts, quickly before the bloke gets back."

I didn't know what he was talking about, but the urgency in Bert's voice compelled me to get up and run after him. We weaved through the windbreaks and beach towels, dodging the sandcastles, making a beeline for the jetty. He ran up the faded, salt-stained wood at full tilt and threw himself off the end and into the sea. Having seen what he was about to do, I, too, sped up the ramp and launched myself into the air, landing next to Bert and surfacing with a laugh. We swam back to shore and repeated the process with appropriate shouts of joy as we flew through the air and splashed into the water.

After completing this for a third time, we started to attract the attention of some of the other kids on the beach. The smaller ones had gathered to watch, some of the older ones had copied us and were throwing themselves from the pier in a steady procession. The jetty had now become the centre of a raucous cacophony of shouting and splashes.

"Oi, get off of there!"

The man in the cap, with the sleeves of his baggy off-white shirt rolled to his elbows, returned from his break. He was in charge of pulling the jetty up and down the beach and was now half-running down the sand, waving his sun-browned arms and shouting at us to get off. As he arrived, one or two brave souls took one last jump into the water while the rest of us scattered to where we had all come from. Me and Bert went back to our towels and sat down laughing.

"That was brilliant," I told Bert.

"You kids, get off of that, it's private property," Bert answered, mimicking the gruff voice and strong local accent of the boatman. We laughed together, and then Bert looked up at the sun, shading his eyes with his hand,

"I'm too hot, shall we go somewhere else?"

"Can't we wait and see if the boat bloke goes away again?"

"He won't go for ages, let's walk down the beach a bit."

I agreed, a bit disappointed that we wouldn't get to dive off the boat ramp again today. We put on our clothes and shoes and walked away, leaving a gap amongst the other people who had made camp on the beach for the day. This would soon be absorbed by the surrounding families and kids, and our presence would be eradicated, it would be as if we had never been there.

The pavement was crowded with hot and bothered visitors sweltering in the heat of the sun, juggling with the conundrum of whether to savour their ice cream or eat it quickly - before it started to dribble down their arms. Sticky children and sweaty parents, all trying to enjoy a day out at the beach after a long, hot drive.

We navigated our way through the hordes, stopping on the way to talk to our friend Pete. He was in my class at primary school, the envy of all of us because his dad had the coolest job ever. Not in the winter, he drove a taxi then, but in the summer when he ran the swing boats, the roundabout and the donkey rides on the beach. Pete was allowed to help him in the holidays. Sometimes, if it was quiet, he would let us have a free go on the brightly painted wooden swings while his dad was busy (we didn't go on the roundabout; that was just for little kids).

We only stayed for long enough to say Hi to Pete; the queues were long, and he was rushing around collecting money and timing how long everybody was on the rides. We watched his dad making a fuss of the three tired-looking donkeys on the sand, bringing them an ice cream tub full of water and checking their saddles and the harnesses with their names painted across their foreheads. The noise and crowds were more intense here than any other part of the beach, we shouted goodbye to Pete and then went off on our way.

We carried on past the lifeboat station, the boating lake and the crazy golf - with its windmill turning lazily and the miniature railway running slowly around its perimeter. At Bert's suggestion, we stopped outside the tiny zoo to see if we could hear the monkeys, but I guess it was too hot even for them. Next, we cut back to the beach, even the section with red flags was crowded today. Nobody was foolish or daring enough to try and swim there, just a few people with their trousers rolled up standing ankle-deep at the water's edge. We carried on walking into the sand dunes.

"Let's go this way," said Bert. He proceeded to clamber to the highest ridge of the sandy hillocks with their patches of tough, sharp grass. I followed him, pausing at the top, I asked why.

"Because Al says sometimes you see people sunbathing topless here."

"What, women?"

"Of course, stupid," he proceeded to walk along the top of the dunes, looking carefully into each small area of flat sand where a semi-naked person might think they had some privacy.

We didn't see any more exposed flesh than we had on the other parts of the beach, although we did see a young couple clamped together in a passionate embrace. The man told us to bugger off when he noticed us looking, so we carried on our way. Eventually, we arrived at the far end of the dunes. This was not the most popular part of the beach as it was the greatest distance away from anything good, even the toilets and ice-cream kiosks were a long walk from here. At the end of the last dune was a steep drop-off with an area of sand at the bottom that was unpopulated. We looked at one another, then ran down it at full speed, our legs barely able to keep up with our downward trajectory, landing in a laughing heap at the bottom.

I was still brushing the sand off me when I saw Bert scrambling back up for another go, I dropped my bag and raced after him. This time, we took a short run-up and launched ourselves from the lip of the precipice, landing with a bump halfway down and rolling the rest of the way to the bottom. I knew we would be going again before we had even come to a stop. I hurried to get back to the top, and we repeated the leap of faith with shouts and whoops that startled passers-by. Several goes later, we sat at the bottom to get our breath back. I had sand in my hair, my mouth, my trousers, my shoes – I'm pretty sure I had sand everywhere. Looking at Bert, I could see that he did too. I wondered if Mum was going to make me have a bath tonight, although I thought probably not, as it wasn't the weekend.

Bert pointed towards the far end of the beach,

"We should go there one day."

I looked down the shore to the red cliffs, where the beach ended. It seemed a ridiculously long way to go for a swim.

"Why," I asked, "did Al say there were topless women there too?"

"Twat," Bert pushed my shoulder, "no, it's where some of the other kids hang out."

"Oh, what, from our year?"

"Some of them, yeah, some of the bigger kids too. It's meant to be a bit of a laugh."

"It's bloody miles."

"That's alright, we'll figure it out."

I didn't give much thought as to how we would figure it out; I just assumed it was a Bert thing that he would forget when his next great idea occurred to him.

"Okay, next time we go swimming then. Shall we get going?"

I kind of wanted to get back soon as I needed the loo. Bert shook his hair, flicking sand everywhere, and then we collected our things from where we had dropped them and started the long walk home.

Mum was still in a good mood that evening after her shopping trip with Dad, so my guess about not having to bathe was correct.

NINE

Bert called at my house as I was finishing collecting up the windfall apples from the lawn, not that there had been any wind, they were just dropping off along with all the desiccated leaves. I still hadn't taken Max for his walk, so Bert came to the park with us. Max was excited to have someone else with him, particularly someone who made a fuss of him and threw his stupid ball as many times as he asked. He'd run up and drop the soggy rubber ball at my feet, and then Bert would pick it up and lob it as far as he could. Max chased it down excitedly, then returned it.

For me, taking Max for his walk was a chore, a daily ritual that I was not allowed to ignore or forget. Sometimes, Dad would come with me, but mostly, it was just me and Max. This was one of the conditions that I had happily and enthusiastically agreed to when I had been told we could get a puppy. Don't get me wrong, I like Max; he's good company when I'm on my own in the house. He will sit happily with me, snuggling down at my feet and wagging his tail like mad when I sneak him upstairs. But walking around the park in the dark and rain – or the blazing heat of summer – has taken the edge off the excitement.

"Your dog's great, I wish I was allowed to have a dog," Bert mused.

"He's alright, I suppose, why don't you ask your mum if you can get one?"

"We can't, we rent the house, we're not allowed to have pets."

This was new to me; I had assumed that everybody lived in houses they had bought. It was the first time I had realised that Bert's house wasn't his.

"Whose house is it then?"

"I don't know, some bloke. He comes round for the money every week; Mum gets mad when she doesn't have enough."

I processed this new piece of information and then asked,

"What shall we do today?"

"I just want to go and look around the shops. Alan's not up yet, so we can't go back to mine."

"I've got a model that needs finishing if you want to help."

"What is it?"

"A Lancaster."

"Cool, let's do that and then go down to town."

"Okay."

I was kind of glad. Mum's brother, my uncle Robert, had decided for some reason that I liked Airfix models. He kept sending ever bigger and more complex ones to me for birthdays and Christmas, and I had to build them because he would ask to see them when he came to visit. I found them super fiddly and didn't always have the patience for them. They never looked quite right at the end, either.

Bert, on the other hand, was made up. He sat in my room and carefully assembled the model, following the instruction sheet diligently and taking care with the amount of glue he was using. He gave me a running commentary on what he was doing while I lay on the bed and kept him informed about the latest gossip and info from my Look-in magazine whilst playing Ziggy Stardust on my portable cassette player.

"I used to have a load of Airfix kits when Dad and Mum lived together," Bert told me, "we had to get rid of them when we moved to the new house."

"Couldn't you have kept them at your dad's house?"

"He said there wasn't space. I think he just didn't want them. He's a bit of a dick, really."

Today was turning out to be a day of revelations, first finding out about rented houses, then hearing someone calling their own dad a dick. I tentatively asked why.

"Because he left us, went off with someone he worked with. Mum was upset; we had to move out of the house, and Mum had to go to work full-time. I hate him."

I think I sort of got it now. I knew this sort of thing happened to people, but this was the first time I had ever really talked to somebody else about it.

"Why did he do that?"

"Because he's a dick, I told you."

That seemed fair enough to me, I was glad my dad wasn't a dick. I changed the subject,

"Are you nearly finished?"

Bert's answer was to turn around and hold up the completed Lancaster. I could manage the transfers myself, so the job was done.

"Thanks, mate."

"No problem, I enjoyed it."

Bert insisted on saying goodbye to Max, and then we went to see what was going on in town. This usually meant reading the magazines in the newsagent until we got thrown out - '*if you're not buying that, put it back*'. From there, we wandered along looking in the shop windows until we got to the big shops. WH Smith and Woolworths had the most browsing potential and offered a chance, even at this early date, to start making a mental note of what would go on my Christmas wish list.

To finish off, I would frequently stop in the second-hand bookshop that was located at the place where the shopping centre started; it was a leftover from the old row of shops that had stood there before. They didn't turn you out as quickly as the newsagent, even though the man in there probably knew we didn't have any money to spend.

When I did have some money, I would quite often buy something from the cheap pile he kept in the corner. The box of random, slightly damaged books that nobody else wanted to buy. He had a far more interesting selection than the library.

The lady in the paper shop was hot and bothered and started on us almost immediately, telling us not to mess up the shelves and to leave them alone if we weren't going to buy anything. We moved on and spent a while looking in Smiths before taking ourselves on to our next port of call, Woolworths, which is where the morning took a turn for the worse.

We had just walked through the front door, past the polished wood with gleaming brass handles, and were going towards the middle of the shop when a hand slapped down on my shoulder. I flinched, turned my head and came face to face with Tubs' menacing grin.

"You two girls looking for baby clothes?" he asked, chuckling to himself.

"Leave us alone, Tubs," Bert said.

"Shut your mouth, or I'll punch your fucking face in," he replied, then turned back to me.

"Get me some sweets."

"I haven't got any money."

"I don't care, get me some fucking sweets," his voice was now a low growl, he leant threateningly in towards me.

"But…how?" I looked at Bert.

"He means nick them," he helped.

"But that's…. that's stealing."

"I'm going out the front to wait for you. Don't piss me off, or you'll be sorry."

I turned back to Bert as Tubs swaggered off, looking at him helplessly. Everyone knew that Woolworths had store detectives whose sole job was to look out for and catch shoplifters. They roamed the aisles constantly, hunting down criminals. You never knew who they were, though, because they dressed as ordinary people.

"Why doesn't he just get some himself?" I asked.

"Because he's been caught before, Alan told me. They keep an eye on him if they see him coming in. Just stuff some in your pockets, and we'll walk out, I'll keep a lookout for you." He tried to look reassuring, glancing up and down the aisle as we approached the confectionary.

I stood in front of the shelves and looked at the brightly coloured wrappers, then glanced along the row. Everybody else seemed to be ordinary shoppers, engrossed in what they were doing, minding their own business and taking no notice of me and Bert. At least, that was how it appeared, but I was sure store detectives wouldn't be walking around in trench coats with magnifying glasses, would they? Any one of them could be waiting to pounce: the old lady with the stick, the man in the straw hat, the lady in the flowery dress. Okay, probably not the two kids who were kneeling on the floor looking at something further down.

After one more glance around, trying - and probably failing - not to look furtive or suspicious, I reached out randomly and grabbed the first thing that came to my hand, putting it straight into my pocket. My heart was pounding, and I felt slightly dizzy, certain that I would now be stopped and taken to the manager's office. From there, the police would come and take me home to face the wrath of my parents.

It didn't happen. I smiled at Bert and then attempted to saunter casually out of the shop without running despite the nearly overwhelming compulsion to do so. By the time I got outside into the sunshine, I was sweating; Tubs stepped forward from the railings he was leaning against to meet me, with a shark-like grin, he draped his arm over my shoulder and guided me away from the shop and around the corner.

As soon as we were out of sight of the entrance, he stopped, turned to face me and held out his hand. I reached into my pocket and pulled out a Fry's Turkish Delight, which he snatched from me with a look of disgust on his face. He tore it open and started to eat it anyway, dropping the wrapper on the floor.

"Next time, get me something fucking decent," he told me through a mouthful of revolting half-chewed, pink chocolate gloop. He turned and walked off, and I let out a breath as my ordeal finally came to an end. Bert, who had been trailing a little way behind us, came over to me.

"You all right?"

"Yeah, fine," I told him, although I thought I might burst into tears at any moment. I was still waiting for someone from Woolies to come running after me. "That was scary, I thought I'd get caught." This was true, but at the same time, I was aware that I was talking too quickly and sounded as excited as I felt at the thrill of doing something forbidden – and not getting caught.

"Did you keep any, or did you give them all to Tubs?"

"I gave it to Tubs. I only got a Turkish Delight."

Bert pulled a face, then reached into his pocket and produced four rolls of fruit pastilles,

"Lucky I got these then, isn't it?" He handed two of the packets of sweets to me as I stood slack-jawed, looking at him.

"Did you….?" I asked.

"Yeah, couldn't let you do it all by yourself, could I? Shall we go and sit somewhere and eat them?"

We doubled back towards the station, walking tentatively as we went back past Woolworths. Outside the grand façade of the train station, we found an unoccupied bench in the shade of the wall. We claimed it for ourselves, sprawling across the wooden slats as we started to eat our booty. The sweets seemed to taste more sugary and more chewy than normal, all the better for being illicit. We watched people coming and going through the arched entrance to the huge Victorian edifice that was the station. It was massively outsized for the single train that ran in and out of it. The town used to be a much more popular destination than it is now.

A steady trickle of people filed into the ticket office. Before long, we heard the train arriving behind us, announcing itself with a series of clanks, clatters, whistles, footsteps and banging doors. This minor commotion was followed by a trail of people leaving the station, walking past us in various interpretations of what would make a good beach outfit. There was no clear consensus: men in flared jeans with no shirt, women in long-sleeved tops and short shorts, the only common factor seemed to be the plethora of hats on display.

The dominant form of head attire for ladies was brightly coloured, wide-brimmed, floppy hats. For men, it was the sort of straw hats that were shaped to look like the sort of proper hats that older blokes wear. I didn't get it myself, surely having something on your head would make you hotter, not cooler?

As I watched the woman in the short shorts pass by, Bert leaned towards me,

"Get up slowly and walk over to the wall by the gates," he said quietly, pointing in the direction he wanted me to go.

"Eh? What?" I responded.

"Come over to the wall, now," he grabbed my arm and half dragged me through the stragglers at the tail-end of the newly arrived passengers, stopping once we were next to the place he had indicated. He put his finger to his lips and pointed through the narrow gap beside the gate that our new angle afforded. At first, I could only see the front of the pub across the road, the Railway Tavern. I was about to ask what I was looking at when the familiar figures of Alan and Tubs came into view. They were laughing as they walked together, which was all I saw before I ducked quickly back behind the wall and out of their sight.

"Shit, that was close," I didn't want to meet Tubs for a second time today and was relieved that Bert had spotted them in time before they saw us.

"Let's follow them, see where they're going," Bert suggested. I couldn't believe it, having narrowly avoided coming into their firing line, Bert now wanted to run the risk of staying close by them. I didn't want to, but before I could say this, Bert was off, out of the station and over the road. I kept up with him and was glad that he was keeping a healthy distance between us and them, at least far enough that we would be able to run away if we were spotted.

Bert's plan very nearly came undone from the start. As Alan and Tubs passed the first house in the row, Tubs paused for long enough to give the doorbell a long, hard ring before they ran on ahead. We had to wait. If anybody had answered, we would have got the blame if we'd been passing.

It was academic; nobody answered, and the older boys did not look behind themselves once as they made a beeline for the alley that bordered the Wilds, clearly making their way to the gap at the end of the fence.

"They're going to the Grotty Grotto," Bert informed me.

"Oh, okay. What shall we do then?" I had assumed that we would not be joining them there.

"Spy on them, of course, just wait a moment until they're in."

I waited nervously, not particularly wanting to go into the Wilds with them. But I had Bert with me, and he seemed to have a plan, which somehow seemed to make it feel safer. After a moment or two, we crept along the edge of the fence in time to see Alan slip and Tubs squeeze through the gap and into the long grass. Bert and I moved cautiously forward, then waited on the other side, listening.

"Ah, you fucking prickle bush," Tubs' voice rang out, followed by the sound of undergrowth being stomped and sworn at. Bert grinned at me, and we waited for a few more moments before we followed their route into the Wilds. We went the same way as we had on our previous visit, arriving at the bunker, where Tessa was still in love with Ian. I followed Bert up onto the roof again, and, keeping low, we made our way to the edge facing the Grotto. There, we lay flat on our stomachs on the hot, rough concrete.

"What if they see us?"

"They won't; if they do, we'll run away. They'll never get up here quick enough to catch us." He pointed down to the Grotto where Alan was just emerging into the clearing, closely followed by Tubs.

It was a reassuringly long way away, although I wasn't sure how much spying we would be able to do if we couldn't hear them. Bert didn't seem bothered. He watched intently as his brother rearranged some crates into a position that allowed him to slouch comfortably, and Tubs clumsily followed suit.

I was going to ask what we would do next now that they appeared to be sprawled out in the sun for the afternoon. Before I could, Alan reached into the bag he had been carrying and took out two small green tins. He passed one to Tubs before pulling the tab on his own and drinking from it. Tubs did the same, swallowing in large gulps with his head tipped back.

"You know what that is, don't you?" Bert asked.

"Drinks," I answered, "I wish I had one." It was hot out in the sun, and I was thirsty.

"Idiot," it's beer.

Now, I peered more intently. I could see that it was the same sort of tins that Dad and his friend Bill sometimes had.

"Where did they get those? They're not old enough."

"He must have nicked them from Dad's. He's going to be in so much trouble when Mum finds out." Bert was very pleased about this, hardly able to hide his relish at the thought. I guessed from his tone of voice that his mum definitely would find out. I looked back to the grotto and saw that Alan had reached into his pocket now, he was passing a cigarette to Tubs before lighting one of his own. He inhaled the smoke and blew it out in a cloud as he handed the matches to his waiting friend.

"He's so for it," Bert chuckled as he saw what was happening.

We watched as they smoked their cigarettes and drank their beer, it wasn't that interesting. I was just about to suggest we leave our scorched perch when Alan reached into his bag once more. He produced a magazine, which he opened up and showed to Tubs. They both became animated and excited. I couldn't see what it was from this distance and was about to ask Bert when he said,

"It's a Playboy, they've got a dirty magazine."

I wasn't completely naïve. I knew what Playboy was. It was one of the magazines with nearly naked ladies that are on the top shelf in the newsagent, the ones that you never seemed to see anybody buy. Now I looked back more carefully, I could see that Bert was probably right, I could make out the figure of a woman on the front cover. They studied it intently, with Tubs at one point snatching it from Alan and rubbing its open pages against his groin as he laughed.

Eventually, as I was at the point of telling Bert I wanted to go now, the magazine was folded back up and put back into its bag, which in turn was pushed deep underneath one of the bushes as Alan and Tubs got ready to leave. This was our cue, we scurried to the far side of the hut and dropped down to ground level, from there, we hurried out of the Wilds and back to the road. We made it out unseen and took ourselves to the park, where we sat in our tree and talked about everything we had just seen.

Later, as the temperature started to reach its peak for the day, we returned to Bert's house for a drink of squash and somewhere cooler to hang out.

TEN

We were slumped in the cool shade of the sitting room in front of the TV when Alan and Tubs arrived back at the house. It might have still been the same cricket match as yesterday that we were watching, I still didn't understand what was going on. Mostly, it seemed to be people talking about how hard it was to keep the pitch in good shape in this extraordinarily hot weather. They kept showing close-ups of the cracks in the mud to prove it. We had turned the sound down low and had the windows wide open to try and encourage the stifling air to move about a bit, so we heard them approaching as they walked noisily up the road.

"I wanna put on a clean shirt before she gets here," Alan's voice wafted into the room.

"Why? That one's okay," answered Tubs.

"Because we're going out now, I wanna look my best."

"Going out where?"

"Not anywhere, going out with each other, pillock."

The front door opened and then slammed shut as they came into the house, still talking loudly.

"Oh yeah, right. Do you think her friend likes me?"

"Dunno, she might if you put on a clean shirt."

The conversation was now moving up the stairs.

"Can I borrow a shirt?"

"I haven't got one that would fit you."

Whatever the answer to that was, it was lost as the bedroom door slammed shut, Bert looked at me and giggled.

"Guess Al's got a girlfriend then."

"Is it that Janet?" I was curious; the concept of girlfriends was fairly new to me, and I didn't understand much about how the process worked.

"Yeah, she's been calling around all the time," Bert rolled his eyes and turned back to watch the cricket. I carried on watching, too, but a bunch of blokes in white trousers standing in a field and occasionally throwing a ball was insignificant compared to the news that Janet was now Al's girlfriend.

Loud music filtered down from upstairs, a lot of guitars and a man screaming. It wasn't as good as my David Bowie tape, although right now, I couldn't imagine anything being as good as that. Despite the volume of the music, I heard laughter through the open window. I looked up to see Janet and Theresa walking past, shortly followed by a knock on the front door.

Bert had seen them, too.

"You get that, Shorts. They'll never hear it upstairs."

"Yeah, alright," I answered. It was fair enough, I was sitting the closest. I got up and opened the front door,

"They're upstairs," I informed the girls before leaving them on the doorstep and returning to my chair in the sitting room. Janet appeared in the doorway,

"Is it okay to go up?" she asked.

"Yeah, follow the noise," answered Bert, pointing at the ceiling and not looking away from the TV. Janet muttered a thank you before turning towards the staircase, leaving Theresa standing smiling in her place. She was wearing a striped dress with no sleeves, and her long hair was tied back in a ponytail again. A swarm of freckles were splashed across her cheeks and nose, and her arms and legs were tanned and brown, with more freckles - along with the remains of some peeling skin - on her shoulders. The deep tans and sunburn were kind of the uniform for us kids that summer.

"Hi Bert, Hi Shorts," she said, inviting herself into the room. Bert raised his hand but otherwise took the least possible interest he could in her arrival. She came and sat on the arm of the chair I was sitting on, so close she was almost touching me with her leg,

"How did you like Ziggy Stardust?" she asked.

"Uh.. oh, yeah, it's really good, I like it."

"That's good, not everybody gets it," she rolled her eyes up and looked at the ceiling where the sound of guitars, drums and wailing was continuing unabated. "Have you heard any of his other stuff?"

"Ah, no, not yet, except Major Tom." That had been played over and over on the radio a couple of years ago. Along with everybody else, I knew it well enough to sing along.

"Oh, Space Oddity's good. Here, you can borrow this if you want, see if you like it."

She reached inside her shoulder bag and passed me a tape. The inlay card was covered in neat, multi-coloured writing that listed the contents. I looked at the spine where 'Transformer' was written in red ink and 'Raw Power' in blue, neither of these titles meant anything to me, they could have been the names of the albums or the names of the bands.

"That's by Lou Reed, it's the one I told you about," Theresa put one red fingernail on the first title, "the other is Iggy and the Stooges." She had leaned closer to me to do this, and a kind of flowery, minty smell wrapped itself around me.

"Thanks," I said, "when do you want it back?"

"There's no rush, any time's fine," she smiled, showing a row of straight white teeth, simultaneously betrayed and enhanced by a wayward, crooked eye tooth. I was about to say something else, although I wasn't sure what it was going to be, when I was interrupted by Tubs shouting down the stairs,

"Oi, are you coming up here?"

He thumped down the steps two at a time and stood in the doorway. Theresa was still facing away from the door; she pulled a face for my benefit before turning around,

"Yes, shall I bring a bucket of water for the lovebirds?"

"If you want," he scowled at me and Bert, "just stop hanging around with the bum boys."

"Leave them alone, they're cute," Theresa admonished as she followed Tubs.

"Bloody bent is what they are," Tubs told her as he went back to the sound of the music, anything else he may have said was cut off by the sound of the bedroom door slamming shut.

"Wanker," Bert mumbled from the sofa.

I agreed with him, although my mind was quite preoccupied by what had just happened. I had talked to girls before, obviously, but they didn't usually come and talk to me about anything much. Generally speaking, the boys and the girls at school kept to their own groups of friends, who mostly happened to be the same gender. But now Theresa, one of the big girls, had talked to me; she had sat near me and smiled at me, and I was beginning to realise I might be missing out on something by just hanging out with the other boys. I wanted to go home and listen to the new tape she had just lent me. I didn't know it then, but in the coming years, tapes like this would become an unofficial currency amongst me and my friends. They would be bartered, traded, and reproduced ad infinitum. But for now, I just wanted to find out what was in this new rectangular plastic box.

"Tubs fancies her," Bert informed me, "he's got no chance."

Like a lot of things Bert told me, I wasn't sure how he knew this. I guessed he had deduced it from the snippets we had overheard earlier. I figured it must be something to do with having a big brother, although given how little he and Alan seemed to talk to each other, even during this uneasy truce their mum had brokered, I wasn't sure how that worked.

The front door opened again, and Bert's mum came in,

"Hello, boys, I see you're busy then. Did you have a good day?"

Bert told her we did. She barely acknowledged his answer before going to the bottom of the stairs and shouting for Alan to 'turn that racket down.' She then came back to the sitting room and asked Bert to go up and tell Alan to turn his music down.

"Then you can give me a hand in the kitchen. I need some spuds peeled for the cottage pie. Is your friend staying?"

I made my excuses and went home to my considerably quieter house.

Dad was home early; he and Uncle Bill were on light duties this week on account of their adventure on the moor and dramatic brush with death. It meant we all had tea together again for a change, which was nice. It also meant that Mum's good mood continued, which was also nice. Even though Dad grumbled that he had spent his whole shift 'just doing paperwork,' I sensed that he was secretly quite pleased with not having to go out putting out fires all day.

After we had finished, I was helping with the dishes, but when Mum and Dad started kissing in the kitchen, I made my excuses and went upstairs to listen to my new tape. I didn't like it – I loved it. The Lou Reed album was fantastic, every bit as good as Ziggy Stardust and the Spiders from Mars. The other side, Raw Power, was not the same, but there was something about it that I liked – I just didn't know what yet. It wasn't Showaddywaddy, that's for sure. I looked through my meagre collection of tapes to decide which I would sacrifice to copy this new one over, pretty much anything was my conclusion.

I sat and read the track titles and was mesmerised by Theresa's meticulous and graceful writing (I assumed it was hers) and decided I would try and copy my inlay card exactly like hers.

***

Janet had called for Theresa again, asking – practically begging, actually – for Theresa to come with her next time she went to see Alan. She had seen him again the previous day, but Tubs had hung around the whole time, talking to Alan or suggesting something they should do every time she started to get close to him. She needed someone (Theresa) to go with her and talk to Tubs, distract him for long enough for Janet to make her move and signal her intentions to Alan.

Theresa's stomach turned at the thought of spending time with those two boys, especially Tubs. But Janet had always been very persuasive; she badgered her until, eventually, she had grudgingly agreed to go along. That had been yesterday, today, she had found herself in the small grassed park in town with Janet and the two boys. She had steeled herself and was doing her very best to talk to Tubs, who in turn was doing his very best to look down her top again. While she half-engaged him in a conversation about the best things to do in town, Janet put her plan into action.

In truth, she practically launched herself at Alan. Wrapping herself around him and planting her mouth on top of his. They stayed like that for some time, Theresa gave up trying to divert Tubs as he turned to watch them, his eyes greedily drinking in what they were doing. Alan began to rub one of his hands up and down Janet's back, under her blouse, and Tubs turned his squinting eyes hopefully towards Theresa. She edged as far down the bench as she could without falling off and desperately tried to think of a way out of the situation she now found herself in.

The problem was resolved when two elderly ladies who were passing by paused long enough to tut and comment out loud about how disgusting it was. Janet and Alan pulled their faces apart, and Alan told the departing backs of the old women to piss off, then suggested to Janet that they go back to his house, so people would stop bothering them. Alan and Tubs started to march off immediately, Janet lingered, walking more slowly as she excitedly told Theresa about the events of the last ten minutes or so. Although Theresa was fully aware of what had happened, she didn't try to dissuade her from talking. At least it was better than listening to Tubs.

The gap between the boys and girls kept widening until Alan turned round and shouted,

"We'll just see you there, shall we?"

"Fine," Theresa yelled back before slowing down even more as Janet continued to fill her ears with protestations of love, lust and desire.

When the front door was opened by Shorts, Theresa felt a surge of relief that there was someone normal to talk to at last. While Janet made a beeline towards the loud music coming from upstairs, she followed Shorts into the front room and sat on the arm of his seat. She asked if he'd listened to the tape she'd seen him with last time and enjoyed his evident pleasure as he answered. She then magicked the one she had made for him from her bag, like Paul Daniels. He seemed to be enthusiastic, and this endeared him to her even more. She had recently found herself in a constant struggle to find anybody who shared her taste in music. Or, more specifically, her distaste for most of the music that was played on the radio at the moment.

Within six months, her search for something different - something new that wasn't just radio junk or heavy metal – would be over. Punk rock would arrive with a snarling roar, and she would find the music that would define her teenage years and stay with her for the rest of her life. For now, she was still trawling the archives of her older sister's record collection, trying to find anything half-decent. Aside from an AC/DC album and a depressing amount of whiney Bob Dylan records, her sister had surprisingly good taste. Theresa had unearthed some great music that she was keen to share if only she could find people who weren't too busy listening to disco shit. Shorts seemed like he might be open to exploring some of her musical discoveries with her, which made her happy.

The conversation was cut short by Tubs, who, after being completely obnoxious to Shorts and Bert, insisted she come upstairs. There he proceeded to try and put his hand on her knee while Janet and Alan attempted to suck each other's faces off on the bed. Eventually, she had had enough; enough of listening to Queen, enough of watching Alan trying to put his hands inside any and every bit of Janet's clothing and enough of Tubs' clumsy and unwanted advances. When the message came from downstairs that it was nearly teatime, she politely made her excuses and walked home.

Janet barely acknowledged her leaving, Alan not at all. Tubs glowered, his face a mixture of petulance and lust. She had been disappointed that Shorts didn't seem to be around anymore when she got downstairs, but she was going straight to her sister's room when she got back to decide what musical offering she should present Shorts with next.

ELEVEN

I was making my way slowly around the park, stopping frequently to pick up the slobber-coated, tooth-marked, faded red ball. I would throw it as far as I could while flop-eared, waggy-tailed Max ran excitedly after it. I had just launched it towards a long downslope to buy myself some time when a voice called out,

"Shorts!"

I looked around and saw Theresa walking towards me. I'm not sure how I hadn't seen her sooner, I guess I had been preoccupied with Max and his stupid ball. Theresa was wearing a floaty white dress, and her hair was loose on her shoulders, she looked like she could pass for a grown-up, she looked beautiful.

"Hi," I managed.

"How did you like the tape?" she asked. She was smiling and seemed genuinely interested in what I thought, but before I could answer, Max came bounding back. He dropped his ball on the path and began running around both of us, jumping up at Theresa to be made a fuss of. I was glad it wasn't muddy, given what a mess Max usually makes when he pesters someone, but I was still worried he would make the white dress dirty, so I called him back. I commanded him to get down in the stern voice Dad had told me to use, but he was having none of it, not while Theresa was obligingly giving him all the attention he desired.

"Oh, Shorts, is this your dog? He's adorable, is that his name, Max?"

He wasn't adorable; he was licking her hand and running between her legs.

"Yeah. Sorry, he's all over-excited."

"Oh, Max, aren't you the sweetest? Come here, you, come on."

She was patting his head and then rubbing his tummy when he lay on his back, and he was lapping it up - until he remembered his ball. He picked it up from where he'd abandoned it and dropped it at Theresa's feet, from where she gingerly picked it up and threw it into the grass.

"The tape was brilliant," I told her in this brief lull, "I really liked Transformer."

"I knew you would," she told me, "I'm going to make you a copy of The Velvet Underground, that was his band in the sixties, you'll love it."

I threw Max's ball again before I answered,

"That'll be great, thanks." In truth, I'd never heard of them, but if yesterday's music was anything to go by, I figured it would probably be okay.

"Okay, well, I've got to go, or I'll be late. See you around, Shorts, see you, Max."

Max was momentarily undecided as to whether to remain loyal and faithful to me or to go off with his new friend. In the end, he stuck with me, probably because I'm the person that feeds him, and we finished our walk with a spring in our steps. Max because he'd been for a walk, and me because….well, I'm not sure. I guess I was just in a good mood.

When I got home, Bert was waiting at the front of my house, leaning against the wall. The twins had come across to talk to him, asking questions about the huge bike with outsized cow horn handlebars that he was standing beside. The frame had been crudely painted with a fresh-looking coat of thick black paint, which was betrayed by the rusted wheel rims and worn tyres. Me and Max stopped to look at the bike, well, Max stopped to run around Bert's legs, say hello to the twins and be made a fuss of, I looked at the bike.

"Cool bike, I didn't even know you had one."

"I don't, it's Al's. He hardly ever uses it, so I've borrowed it."

"Won't he mind?"

"He won't know, he's gone out."

"Great, I'll get mine, and we'll go for a ride."

Bert held up a carrier bag,

"Get your trunks, we're going to the beach."

"Okay, give me a minute."

I wasn't sure why we'd go to the beach when we've got bikes to ride, you can't take them on the sand, they get all messed up. I didn't question it, though, I went inside, gave Max some water, found my swimming things and collected my bike from the garden. I met Bert at the front of the house, and we cycled down the road, Bert riding confidently despite the bike being too big for him.

I had assumed we were going directly to the seafront, but I was wrong. Bert led me up the steep hill – where we both had to get off and walk the last third and towards the cut-through that led to the far end of the seafront, the cliffs. I tried asking him where we were going, even though I had guessed by now, but he kept answering, 'You'll see'. We had to concentrate in the cut-through; it's fairly narrow, and you have to be ready to stop and navigate around anybody who happens to be walking that way. This is usually accompanied by admonishments to *'go carefully there boys'* and to *'watch what you're doing, somebody's going to get hurt with you racing around like that'*.

Nobody did get hurt, though, and we made it to the long, straight, single road that leads to the cliffs. The road and the beach both end there, the only way to go after that is up the cliff path or turn back the way you came. There is a space at the end where you can leave bikes off the road and not on the sand. I was encouraged to see several other bikes there, but when I looked down to the beach, I couldn't see any of the expected groups of boys.

"Where is everyone then?" I asked Bert.

"You'll see, get your trunks on."

Bert was already half undressed and had wrapped his towel around his waist to change into his black Speedos. I hurried to catch up but was still way behind him as he splashed into the sea and started swimming parallel to the cliff towards the point. I briefly thought again about Kevin Freeman and Mum's dire warnings about only swimming in the right places. I was pretty sure Kevin hadn't been swimming at this end of the beach when he drowned, so it was probably okay.

The point juts out into the sea at the end of the beach, reaching out to the open ocean. When the tide is out, you can simply take off your shoes and socks and walk around the end to an isolated, secluded bay, which is popular for people who want a less crowded beach to sit on. I found out a few years later that it was also popular for teenagers who wanted a quiet and undisturbed place to have an evening bonfire and some illicit alcohol, but that's a whole other story.

Today, the tide was in, and I swam to the rocky ledge that you could climb onto to scramble around the point rather than swimming the whole way. Bert was waiting for me, beads of water glistening on his body. He flicked his long dark hair back out of his eyes, then watched as I clambered up the well-worn handholds and out the sea. Together, we continued along the orange rocks towards the very tip of the point. Now I could hear the voices of other kids, so Bert hadn't gone stark-staring mad after all, they were here somewhere. There is a higher ledge that overhangs the one we were traversing, below us, a kid I knew from school was climbing out of the water onto the slippery rocks.

"Hi, Bert," he said.

Bert replied with a smile,

"How is it?"

"Brilliant, I'm going back up."

Just as he finished speaking, there was a shout, and a body from the higher ridge plummeted past us, landing in the sea with a splash. I was startled and looked at Bert and the other kid, then back to the sea, where I saw a tousled head of wet hair being shaken by a boy who was laughing as he swam the short distance to the rocks. I realised then what was going on.

The secluded cove, which could only be reached at low tide from the beach, had another way that it could be accessed. A series of rickety stairs, ladders and steps led to the top of the cliff, from where the brave souls that took this route could follow a steep clifftop path back to the main beach. I could see the first set of steps now we were at the point. The kid who had spoken to Bert climbed halfway up them, then ducked under the handrail and onto the higher ledge where the other kids were gathered. I followed Bert as he ascended the rusted iron steps to the ridge.

As we stepped onto the red sandstone, dark and wet with the drips and footprints of the jumpers who had gone before us, the first people we saw were Alan and Tubs. My heart sank, and Bert's face changed from the delighted glow of earlier to a scowl.

"What are you two benders doing here?" Alan asked.

"Same as you, going swimming."

"You know what Mum will say when I tell her you were here, don't you?"

"Nothing, because then she'd know you were here too."

Alan's face contorted as he tried to work out how to resolve this dilemma. Eventually, he concocted a strategy,

"Just stay out of my way, you little fart, or I'll thump you."

"Yeah, and I'll help him, you little faggots," Tubs added, "you'll be too wimpy to jump anyway."

Bert took the challenge, he turned and walked directly to the edge where, to the whoops and hollers of the other boys, he leapt into the sea fifteen feet below without a moment's hesitation. I watched, frightened that the next time I saw Bert, he would be a bloody mess on the rocks below. I leant over the railing of the steps until I saw him coming back up, dripping and grinning.

"Your turn now, Shorts, it's brilliant."

Behind me, another boy launched himself from the cliff, even the thought of someone else doing it made me feel cold despite the bright sunshine. I knew that I wasn't going to be able to do this. Bert joined the back of the ragged and informal queue by the cliff face, and I stood by him, watching each consecutive boy take his turn before eventually returning to the back of the line with a smile on his face. As we inched nearer to the front, my hands bunched into tight fists, and my body felt tense and stiff.

And then it was us.

"Just have a look over the edge," suggested Bert, "it's not so bad. If you don't want to do it, you can just hang out with the other kids who aren't keen." There were indeed some bystanders who appeared to have no intention of jumping, leaning against the rocks at the rear of the ledge and shouting encouragement and cheers for those who were actively involved. Amongst that group was Tubs, a tee shirt pulled tightly over his rounded torso and the ever-present sneer on his face. I did what Bert had suggested and inched my way forward to the precipice, leaning forward to look down at the gently lapping waves and the jagged rocks, and I knew I couldn't do it. I was turning round to retreat and tell Bert he could go before me when I felt hands push against my back, hard enough to send me flying over the edge.

Everything was slow and quick at the same time. I felt myself falling through the air towards the rocks; I knew I was screaming even though I couldn't hear it. I braced myself for the inevitable impact as I tumbled closer to the swelling green wavelets, in that moment, I could see the glittering reflection of the bright summer sun in each ripple. Frozen in a brief moment. Then I hit the water. My open mouth gulped in some salty brine, and I couldn't tell which way was up and which was down. I wondered if this was what it was like for the Freeman kid. Had he felt the caustic rasp of the seawater in his throat and the seaweed grasping at his ankles and pulling him down in his last moments of fear and panic? The disorientation was brief, and I found myself breaking the surface, coughing and spluttering. I looked for the direction of the rocks so I could climb ashore.

As I reached the slippery, wet crevice that was the exit point, I saw a hand reaching down. I looked up and saw Bert's face; he was looking directly at me with no trace of a smile.

"God, are you okay, Shorts?" he asked.

I looked down, examining my shivering body and realised that I was unscathed, with no blood or mangled limbs, then I started to laugh.

Bert sat next to me while I got my breath back. The sun dried off the seawater, and I realised that I felt great - surviving the fall had been more exhilarating than I could have ever predicted.

"That was great; I'm going to do it again. But why did you push me?"

Bert looked shocked,

"I didn't, it was Tubs. The other big kids are giving him hell, listen."

I listened, and from above, I could hear raised voices, mostly profanities. In the midst of them, I could hear Tubs protesting, but he was being shouted down by the other boys. A couple of the big kids had joined me and Bert; they had come down to check I was okay, and I assured them I was. They accompanied us back up the steps to the ledge, where I was greeted with a cheer and some pats on the back. I felt like a hero, and when I told everyone I was going to do it again, they respectfully moved out of the way, temporarily suspending the queueing system. So now I was committed. I was still scared, who wouldn't be? But I knew I could survive it, and besides, everyone was watching expectantly now. I stepped to the edge and, with only the briefest of glances down, threw myself forward and let gravity do its thing.

As the afternoon went on, me and Bert worked our way through the line several more times. I found myself enjoying the feeling of falling safely. Tubs stayed firmly at the back of the ledge, occasionally being teased by Alan and some of the other big kids about being too much of a chicken. He protested, of course, claiming a raft of reasons why he wasn't going to do it right now and that he would jump later. He never did, though, although he told Alan several times that he was going to do it in a minute once all the stupid little kids were out of the way. He looked pointedly in mine and Bert's direction when he said this.

I don't know how long we spent there, but it came to an end when one of the big kids came up the steps and told the rest of us,

"I hit the bottom that time; I think the tide's going too far out now."

There were some groans from the other boys, but he was right, the tide had receded some way from when we had arrived. The biggest kids seemed to hold some authority regarding policing what was okay and what was not. In ones and twos, everybody climbed back down the steps or took one last leap, like a line of lemmings, before starting the swim back to the beach. Along with a couple of others, me and Bert went back up for one last jump, but it really was starting to get too shallow, my feet hit the sand under the water the last time I jumped. Together, we began our journey back to the beach, I was excited after the exhilaration of conquering my initial fears – albeit with Tubs' help, and was talking about coming again next time the tide was high enough.

First swimming, then wading, and lastly paddling, we arrived back at the main beach. It was now in the shadow of the cliff as the sun's position had changed. We ran back up to our piles of clothes and started to dress. It didn't occur to us to stay on the beach any longer – what interest or excitement could it possibly hold for us now, after the thrill of cliff jumping?

With my sandy clothes sticking to my wet body, I turned to walk back to the road, and there were Alan and Tubs. They were standing with their hands on their hips and their arms folded, respectively, with the same unpleasant expressions that had accompanied previous incidents, everything else started to go out of focus, and I barely noticed Bert turning to see them, too.

"Right couple of Tarzans, you two, eh?" Alan smirked, then looked at Bert, "how did you get down here?"

Bert said nothing, just glared back, so Alan helped him out,

"You came on my bike, didn't you? You nicked it, you little prick."

"No, I borrowed it. I didn't think you'd mind because you weren't using it."

"Well, I am now."

"But I'll have to walk back."

Alan stepped forward threateningly with his fists clenched,

"Not my problem, do you want to make something of it? I'm going to murder you if you've scratched the paint anyway."

Bert backed down quietly. Tubs, who had been standing slightly behind Alan smirking, now stepped forward, too.

"I'm going to need to borrow your bike," he told me.

"You can't," I said, "I'm not allowed to lend it."

"Not allowed? Who's going to stop me?"

"My Dad'll be cross if he finds out."

"Don't tell him then, stupid," answered Tubs. Then, with no warning at all, he stepped forward and punched me in the face. Surprised, I fell backwards onto the sand, ending up sitting on the sand with Tubs standing over me. He came forward again and bent down towards me. I was scared he was going to hit me a second time and turned my face away from him, he reached out to the back of my head and pushed me down, forcing my face fully into the sand, it went into my mouth and nose and for a moment I thought I wasn't going to be able to breathe. Then the pressure was gone, and I sat back up, spitting, spluttering and rubbing my eyes. Tubs leant towards me, so close I could smell his fetid breath,

"Your dad will probably burn to death in a fire anyway. It's a shame he didn't the other day."

Then he laughed at his witticism, a loud and semi-snarled laugh that made his body wobble underneath his wet tee shirt. He rejoined Alan, and together, they walked up to the bike park at the end of the road. I sat on the beach crying, feeling the hot tears and snot washing tracks through the sand crusted on my face, and my eye starting to swell and close up. I don't know how long I sat like that, it felt like forever. Also, I didn't know which was the worst: being punched, having my face pushed into the sand, crying in front of Bert, having my bike nicked or the things he had said about Dad. Bert put one of his arms across my shoulders, causing me to flinch momentarily. Realising it wasn't a returning Tubs, I leant into him and let him use the corner of his towel to gently wipe the sand from my face. I was glad he was there, and I was glad he was my friend.

The walk back was long, hot and dusty. I was preoccupied with what Dad would do when he found out I'd had my bike stolen and what Mum would say when she saw my swollen eye. I didn't think it would be anything good. I knew I couldn't tell them what had happened without them knowing where I'd been. If that happened, I probably wouldn't be allowed out for the rest of the holiday. I also knew that was a likely outcome even if they didn't find out what I'd been up to.

Bert was mostly engaged in an expletive-laden monologue describing his brother. His creative use of swear words, many of which I'd never even heard before, was impressive. When I asked him what I should say about my eye, he suggested that I tell them we were playing football, and the ball hit me in the face. This seemed like a plausible excuse to me, even though I didn't usually like playing football. I was fairly sure Mum didn't know that, so I settled on it as it was the best I had.

In the end, I needn't have worried about the bike. Tubs had abandoned it on the pavement outside Bert's house. I collected it and then said goodbye to him, slowly wheeling my bike the remainder of the distance home, anxious about what was going to happen next.

Nothing happened next. Mum saw my eye when she got home and asked what had happened. I told her the football story, and she tutted and rolled her eyes before going to start the tea. I don't know why she didn't ask me loads of questions and make a fuss about it; I can only guess that she was still in a good mood with Dad being home more. She switched the radio on in the kitchen as Queen finished singing about being someone's best friend, followed by the presenter, who began talking about droughts, supply shortages, and only using essential water. This was, I felt, a good thing on balance as it meant I would probably not be told to have a bath. I went upstairs and sat quietly, trying in vain to cool down in my hot and humid room. I decided that the good bits of the day made it okay overall - but the bad bits were shit.

***

Despite her dislike of some of the stupid fashions in girl's clothes, Theresa liked her white dress. She thought it made her look more adult, plus it was comfortable and not too frilly or flowery. She decided to wear it today as she was going to meet her sister, Claire, in town. In one of her frequent outbursts of sisterly affection, Claire had suggested Theresa could meet her for a drink in a café when she was on her break. Claire knew that Theresa would be on her own a lot this summer, with mum and dad both having to go to work and had been trying to make some time for her little sister.

Unlike many of her friends, who had siblings of roughly their age, it was rare for her and Claire to fall out, maybe because there were five years between them. When she heard about some of the fights and feuds that went on in other households, she was quite surprised and a little shocked. She was going to miss her sister in the autumn when Claire was due to go off to university in Bristol - A-level results permitting. Having Claire around had been like having a second mum sometimes. A younger, trendier mum that she could do stuff with, like listening to records and meeting up for drinks in town.

They took their seats in the crowded café, and Theresa perused the menu, even though she knew what she was going to have - a Coke and a slice of cake. She enjoyed being treated like an equal, an adult and was always careful not to embarrass or let her big sister down in any way.

"You've got all hair on the front of your dress," Claire pointed out as they waited for their food.

Theresa told her about bumping into Shorts in the park and his adorable dog, Max. This led to some mild teasing about her having a boyfriend. She felt herself blush and looked away,

"It's not like that. He's younger than me, and he's a boy, so we probably won't be friends next year. But I like him, he's funny. Kind of cute too - but not in a fancying sort of way."

Claire immediately became serious,

"Sorry, I didn't mean to upset you."

"It's okay; I just don't fancy him like that. I don't want to be his girlfriend, just his friend."

"Well, do it then. Nobody else can tell you who you can like or not like, it doesn't matter if he's in the year below you, if he's a boy or if he's a three-headed alien from Mars, it's nobody else's business. Although, if he is a three-headed alien from Mars, maybe don't bring him round the house just yet – Mum would have a fit."

Theresa laughed, she smiled back at Claire and wondered what she would do when her sister left home. She hoped it might involve having a bigger bedroom but wasn't brave enough to ask about that just yet.

TWELVE

I didn't want to go round to Bert's house the next day, mainly because I was worried that Tubs would be there again - I didn't want to see him any time soon. I stayed at home the following day, too, I was messing around in my room, drawing pictures on a half-roll of lining paper that had been left over from when Dad decorated the sitting room at Easter. Rather than tear it into individual pieces, I was creating a continuous sequence of drawings that rolled up on itself as I extended it. My current project was a meticulous copy of a photo of an Egyptian sarcophagus from the encyclopaedia that was propped open in front of me.

There was a knock on the door, and I ran downstairs to open it. Bert was standing outside with a grin on his face.

"Hi, I thought I'd come round here today, is that okay?"

"Yeah, come in. I didn't come round yours because…."

Bert helped me out,

"Because you didn't know if Tubs would be there, I don't blame you. Your eye looks cool, by the way."

I was glad he said that I had been admiring it in the bathroom mirror earlier. A purple lump around the side of my eye with slightly yellowing edges. Mum had tutted at it but said nothing, Dad had not even seemed to notice it. I'm not quite sure what I was proud of, I certainly hadn't come out of the situation with any kind of glory, maybe it was just the thrill of having survived.

"Wow, is all that paper yours? Where did you get it from?"

"Dad got it for me," Bert had seen the roll of paper, he was now unfurling it and looking through the various illustrations that filled every small space from edge to edge.

"Did you draw all these? They're really good."

"Thanks," I was pleased that my handiwork had earned Bert's approval, I had never shown it to anybody else before and had no idea if it was any good or not, I just enjoyed doing it. It was a calming and thoughtful activity when you just wanted to be by yourself for a bit or fill in some time when there was nothing else to do.

"Can I draw on it?"

"Sure," I rolled my half-finished sarcophagus from earlier up for later, then shared out the coloured pencils so that we could sit on either side of the paper and work at the same time. Over the next hour, a battlefield full of ruined buildings, tanks, bomber planes, and heavy artillery gradually emerged in front of us, complete with a selection of soldiers engaged in vicious and bloody conflict. Huge explosions and scenes of combat were rendered in loving detail, with occasional references to my Commando comics to ensure authenticity. Bert's bits weren't as detailed as mine, but I didn't care too much, it was good fun sharing a project with him.

As we drew, we started to create a narrative around the scene. A convoluted tale of danger, heroism and violent, bloody conflict. The battle finally ended with me and Bert joining forces to defeat a mutual enemy. They were ensconced in a towering castle perched on top of a mountain that we had to scale before ensuring our victory. I looked down at what we had achieved together and was taken aback by the scale and scope of our work. Bert repeatedly pointed out the sections – mine and his – which he felt were particularly good, and I felt a certain pride in our joint venture.

Leaving the paper unrolled on the floor, we went down to the kitchen and scavenged some food from the fridge while planning what we would do next. Bert's house was still not a viable proposition, as it was one of the places we would be most likely to encounter Tubs. This left a return visit to the beach, exploring the Wilds again or going down to the town, to the shops. We both decided that the shops were the best option, even though we had no money to spend.

Making sure to pull the door closed behind me, we left the semi-cool of the house for the heat of the day. We ran through the various highlights of the earlier battle as we walked, occasionally ducking behind walls or lampposts when we reenacted engagements with enemy troops. By the time we got to the town centre, we were hot and sweaty, by unspoken agreement, we directed ourselves to the gardens that surround the war memorial, here, there are trees that provide shade and benches to sit on – if you can find one free.

We were lucky, as we approached, a family vacated one of the seats, putting their picnic rubbish in the bin as they left. We moved in quickly and claimed it for ourselves, although the shade was not as good as it could have been as the horse chestnut trees had already started to lose their dried-up leaves. It was going to be a poor conker season this Autumn.

The other benches were all occupied, as well as the wall around the edge and areas of the patchy, yellow grass that were lucky enough to be in the small amount of protection that the shade of the trees offered. We were sitting watching the grockles come and go, pointing out particularly amusing hats, colourful outfits and a family with three kids – all loaded with beach equipment, who were trying to find their way to the seafront.

We were looking over at a girl having a meltdown tantrum because she had dropped her ice cream when someone approached from behind. They swept round the end of the bench and sat themselves beside Bert. At the same time, I became aware that the same thing had happened to me. A warm body nudged up against my hip, and Theresa said,

"Budge up, Shorts, you can't have all the bench." She smiled at me, and I moved along a little to make space for her. Beside me, Bert was telling Janet that he didn't know where Alan was today; he hadn't seen him since that morning, and they weren't talking anyway.

"Why not?" asked Janet.

"Because he's a shit," came the reply.

"Oi, you can't talk about my boyfriend like that," Janet admonished, although it felt a little half-hearted. Theresa laughed, and I thought I liked the sound of her laughing and that I wouldn't mind if she did it again.

"Still listening to your tapes, Shorts?"

"I am, they're really good, thanks for the lend. I've made copies of them now, so I'll give them back to you. Shall I leave them at Bert's house?" I didn't tell her about how I had painstakingly copied out the track lists to make them look as much like her original as I could manage.

"No, hold on to them for a moment, I can lend you some more if you want."

I did want. I wanted to hear more of whatever wonderful new music Theresa was going to bring to me. I also wanted an excuse to see her again, maybe even to hear her laugh if I was lucky. An idea occurred to me.

"I could go to the shop and get some blank tapes now, and then I won't have to keep borrowing yours."

"Okay, do you want us to wait here?"

"Yeah, save our bench for us."

By now, Bert had finished whatever he had been talking to Janet about, probably Alan, and was looking at me with his eyebrows raised and his head at a slight angle. Before he could say anything, I got up,

"Come on, Bert, it won't take a minute. Do you two want a drink?"

"Yes, please," the girls answered in unison.

"Okay, see you in a bit," I started to walk towards the shops, Bert got up and followed me. As soon as we were out of earshot of the bench, he stopped and turned to face me,

"I thought you didn't have any money."

"I don't," I shrugged and carried on walking.

After our encounter with Tubs at Woolworths, I was intrigued by the idea that you could just help yourself to things from shops. I had made one or two trips into town on my own to experiment with this concept.

To be fair, I had tried to cadge some money off of Mum first. I had made her a mug of coffee without being asked, but she had rumbled me straight away,

"What've you done now?"

"Nothing, I just thought you'd like a coffee."

"Why?"

"Because, um, well, you know.."

"No, I don't know. What are you after?"

"Can I have some money, please?"

"Haven't you got any of last week's left?"

Dad used to give me some pocket money each Saturday, but that was long gone.

"Um, well, no, I don't think so."

"You don't think so? Have you or haven't you?"

This was going terribly. We seemed to have got off the subject of whether I could have some money and onto an entirely different topic.

"No."

"Well, you need to be careful, you need to make sure you have enough money left. What did you spend it all on anyway?"

"Stuff."

"Stuff?"

"Things I needed."

"What things? Did you spend it all on sweets?"

"Not all, no."

Actually, that had been most of it, but best not to admit that.

"What then?"

"I can't remember."

So, in the absence of any funds, helping myself seemed like the best option. I had been rewarded with some sweets, a couple of pens and a jug. I wasn't sure what I was going to do with the jug, but it had been in a convenient place for me to pick up and put into my pocket. Maybe I would save it for Mum's birthday. Nobody seemed to notice me as I perused the shop, made my selections, walked towards the cash desk and then calmly walked out of the shop with my loot. I felt emboldened, ready for the big time.

"Are you going to shoplift it?" Bert asked incredulously.

I shrugged again as I turned into Boots. Once inside, I made a show of looking at several things I wasn't interested in to cement my credentials as a bona fide customer. I moved slowly towards the rear of the shop, where the tapes would be. Once I was in front of the shelves, I calmly selected a pack of three Memorex cassettes and slipped them into my pocket. I say calmly, in fact, I was still as terrified as I had been the first time - with Tubs' Turkish Delight. I wanted to get a five-pack, but I could see immediately that they would create an abnormally large bulge in the front of my shorts.

Next, I went to the drinks and picked out two tins of shandy. Bert followed me as I walked up and past the cash register, down the next aisle and out of the shop.

"Bloody hell, Shorts," he said as he looked back over his shoulder towards the shop entrance. "You'll be in real shit if you get caught, you know."

I did know that, the thought scared me to death. But I also knew that the feeling of walking out and nothing happening was electric, I'd felt the same thrill every time I had done it. I smiled at him,

"It's okay, I didn't get caught, did I?" I held up the tins of drink and started to march back towards our bench, hoping that Janet and Theresa would still be there – mostly Theresa.

They were. We plopped ourselves back down on the bench, and I handed the tapes and one of the cans of shandy to Theresa. I opened the other, took a sip and passed it to Bert, Theresa shared hers with Janet. It was maybe one of the sweetest, nicest drinks I had ever had, sat between my best friend and Theresa in the sunshine, with nothing that we needed to rush off and do. I was savouring the moment when I looked down and saw a ladybird land on my knee. I was going to brush it off. Instead, I let it crawl onto the back of my hand and showed it to Theresa.

"Aw, hello, ladybird," she said,

"Yuk, keep that bug away from me," added Janet.

I brushed it off of my hand, then noticed another one, this time on Theresa's shoulder.

"You've got one too, do you think they know each other?" I asked, brushing it off for her. She laughed, then pointed to my legs where two more had alighted, one on my shoe and one on my shin. I started to look around and realised that they were on all of us. Bert had two on his shoulder, and Janet had one on her chest that she was trying to brush off with her chin tucked down so she could see what she was doing. There were several more on the bench, and Theresa had one in her hair.

"You've got one in your hair," I told her.

"Ugh, where?"

"Just there," I pointed for her. Instead of trying to remove it herself, she tipped her head towards me,

"Will you get it out for me?"

I obliged, gently pulling it from her hair, which ran through my fingers like fine silk. We brushed, flicked and picked ladybirds for the next couple of minutes until the onslaught seemed to be slowing down. I looked up and around the garden, and it appeared that everybody else had been similarly afflicted. People were brushing one another's shoulders and hair, sweeping their hands down themselves and checking each other front and back.

Past the grass area, near the shops, a figure was standing next to the trunk of one of the trees. He was looking directly across the open space towards us. Unbothered by what was going on around him, Tubs seemed to be focused intently on Janet, Theresa, Bert and me. When he saw that I had noticed him, he turned quickly and disappeared behind a group of foreign students who had happened to swarm by at that particular moment.

I turned my attention back to the others, who had not seen him. Janet was getting ready to go,

"I'm going to see if I can find Alan, thanks for the drink." She stood up and looked at Theresa, waiting for her to follow. As she got to her feet, another ladybird landed on her cheek, she laughed and brushed it off,

"Well, even Alan can't be as much of a pest as these, thanks for the drink, Shorts. I'll put something you'll like on here for you," she held up the tapes before slipping them into her bag and following Janet across the gardens.

Me and Bert made our way back towards my house, stopping to look at clusters of ladybirds that had congregated on bushes and were intermittently flying from place to place.

"It's like flying ant day, isn't it!" Bert observed.

I agreed, it was like the day of high summer when all the ants synchronised their young queens to go out into the world and look for new homes to start fresh colonies. Those days were weird, what with the waves of insects and flocks of seagulls – who subsequently staggered around drunkenly on the roads. But this was weirder.

***

When Claire came into her bedroom and asked her what was up, it was all Theresa could do to stop herself from crying again. Her day had started okay, Janet had called around and suggested they go for a walk into town. There was no apparent ulterior Alan motive, just a look around the shops and see who else was hanging out. She was glad to have something to do and someone to do it with, funny how you looked forward to the holidays so much, then when they came you didn't know what to do with yourself.

After completing a circuit of the main shopping centre, including a stop into Smiths to say a brief hello to a busy Claire, they had spied two familiar figures sitting on a bench in the gardens by the war memorial, Theresa had suggested they joined them in the hope of getting some normal conversation. Janet had been talking non-stop about Alan from the moment she arrived at Theresa's house. She had been eager to elicit Theresa's opinion about how far she should 'let him go'.

Theresa's opinion was that she should run a mile and not look back. She didn't share that particular notion with Janet but did counsel her to take it slowly and not be pressured into doing anything she didn't want to do. She didn't think Janet would take any more notice of that advice than she would have done to her initial thoughts, but she offered it anyway. Janet continued to tell her every detail of what she and Alan had been up to. A chance to talk to Shorts, however brief, would be a welcome change.

The conversation with Shorts had culminated with him and Bert going off to get some blank tapes. Bert had looked confused, but Shorts led him away with a promise to be back soon. Once they were out of earshot, Janet became very animated, telling her that she had managed to find out Alan's possible whereabouts from Bert. She was all for going straight there right away, but Theresa insisted that they should stay put, at least until the boys got back. Inwardly, she sighed, her morning out with Janet had now, predictably perhaps, turned into another Alan pilgrimage. She decided she would leave them to it today, another hour or two of leering from Tubs would drive her mad. Janet was so focused on Alan that she hadn't even noticed that any of this had been happening, or if she had, she was deciding to ignore it. She was just deciding how to tell Janet this when Shorts got back, loaded with drinks and blank tapes.

She wasn't sure how she knew, but she was fairly certain that he had stolen both the tapes and tins of shandy. She couldn't know for certain, of course, but that was her intuition, and it added a small frisson of excitement to the exchange. She wondered what else she didn't know about Shorts and decided then and there that she would follow her sister's advice. Sod what anyone else thinks, she liked him, and she wanted to find out more about him. He was kind of funny, definitely cute and very unassuming. When she thought about how Bert and Shorts managed to just sit and have a normal conversation, compared to how hard Alan and Tubs had tried to impress her and Janet the other day, it cemented that decision in her mind.

That was the last good part of the day. The swarm of ladybirds that had interrupted them had been disgusting. She didn't normally mind ladybirds; they're kind of cute. But not like that, hundreds of them crawling in her hair and flying around in a swarm like a biblical plague. It heralded the end of their time in town as Shorts and Bert went off to do whatever it was they were up to. She didn't know what it was, but she kind of wished she was going with them. Instead, she followed Janet in the direction of Alan's newly revealed location.

Before they arrived at their destination, Theresa made her excuses, telling Janet that she had agreed to meet her sister later. It was a lie, but Janet was too single-minded in her determination to find Alan to know or care if this was true, she merely gave her a cheery goodbye and then hurried on to find him – leaving Theresa free to walk home alone.

She now had a bit more of a spring in her step. When she got back, she decided she was going to listen to some music, do some drawing, make a new tape for Shorts and drink squash in the back garden. This felt like it would be an ideal afternoon on what was another stiflingly hot day. She left the busy shopping area and started the long walk home via the back roads and shortcuts, taking a familiar route that she knew well.

As she approached the gates to the park, an integral part of the optimum route home, she saw a familiar and unwelcome figure leaning against the railings. She recognised Tubs' red hair and bulky physique from a distance and hesitated, she had no desire to talk with him but also didn't want to take the long, steep detour around the edge of the park. She decided to grit her teeth and run the gauntlet. As she got closer, she could see that Tubs was watching her as she moved towards him, he was sweaty and red-faced, as if he had been running, with dark stains in the armpits of his already grubby shirt.

He looked this way because he had been running. He had followed Janet and Theresa as they moved through the town, telling himself that he would deal with Shorts later. Bert would be trickier, seeing as he was Al's brother, but he would find a way. He guessed that they were going to look for Alan, he decided he would let them find him, then arrive all unannounced and unexpectedly just after the girls did. His plan faltered when the girls split up. Forced to make a choice, he decided to follow Theresa – after all, she was supposed to have been his girlfriend, wasn't she?

Guessing where she was going, he took a different route, running along a parallel road to get ahead of her and meet her by the park. He didn't want to run; he always felt self-conscious of his bulk as he tried to stop his shirt from riding up his stomach and his tits from wobbling. It was when they started doing PE at secondary school that people started to call him Tubs. He hated it at first, more than one person got a black eye or bloodied nose for using the name in his earshot. But nicknames have a way of sticking, so he eventually decided to just go along with it, even though it still rankled sometimes.

As Theresa passed through the gate, he pushed himself off the railings and began to follow her, quickening his pace until he was walking alongside her. At first, he said nothing, just stayed parallel with her, while Theresa did her best to ignore him. Finally, she cracked,

"Hi, Tubs."

He smiled, a kind of lopsided smile that showed his unbrushed teeth in their full, disgusting glory.

"Hi Theresa, are you going somewhere?"

"No, I've been out. I'm just on my way home."

"I'll walk with you if you want."

"Thanks, but I'm okay," Theresa replied. Tubs continued to walk beside her regardless, moving slightly closer as he spoke.

"Did you see anyone while you were out?" he asked, there was something in his tone that Theresa didn't like.

"Not really, just looked around the shops with Janet."

"You should have said, I'd have come with you."

Theresa couldn't think of anything worse - apart from what was happening right now, maybe. She altered her course slightly to keep the distance between her and Tubs, and he made a similar adjustment to close it again.

"We should go out sometime, me and you. You know, without Alan and Janet. Like a date."

Now, Theresa could think of something worse. She wasn't sure what she should say to politely but clearly indicate that she wasn't interested.

"Probably not," she answered, "I've kind of already got a boyfriend."

This last bit was true; she had been seeing a boy in her year for the last couple of months. It had been a bit on and off as he lived in one of the outlying villages, making it difficult to meet up regularly outside of school. She had been thinking about finishing with him when term started again, although she had her suspicions that he was already seeing someone else anyway. Tubs' expression changed, his brow creased, and the attempt at a smile dropped from his lips. He stepped forward quickly and turned to block her way.

"You can finish with him. I bet he's a little squirt. I can beat him up, and then I can be your boyfriend instead."

Theresa's mind raced, how the fuck did Tubs think going out with someone worked? Even with her limited experience, she knew that he was a million miles out. They had neared the gate at the top of the park now, reaching the narrow gap that led to the top gate and her road. Tubs had stopped in the middle of the path and turned to face her. She tried to manoeuvre around him, unsure how to respond to his last comment. As she started to pass between him and the wall, he turned his body towards her and pushed himself against her, trapping her between him and the wall.

She froze with panic as his sweaty weight kept her pinned in place, and his face loomed towards hers, then turned her head to one side. It was just in time; she could smell his breath as his lips started to roughly kiss her cheek and neck, and he increased the contact between their two bodies. Her alarm grew when she felt his hand. He had pushed it up between them and was squeezing her breast roughly as if it were a tennis ball, and he was trying to crush it.

"Get off, get off me. You're disgusting, leave me alone!" she yelled. This probably wouldn't have made any difference, but at that moment, an old lady with a tiny dog on a red lead came through the top gate.

"Are you okay, dear?" she asked.

At the sound of her voice, Tubs stepped back, and Theresa took her opportunity to escape. She ran in the direction of the gate as fast as she could, not looking back or slowing down until she was safely back inside her own house. Behind her, she heard Tubs shout,

"I'll see you tomorrow then."

Then, fading as she increased the distance, she heard him speak to the old lady with the dog,

"You can sod off, you old cow, before I piss on your dog."

She sat in her room and cried, unable to do anything for the rest of the afternoon, terrified that Tubs would come knocking on the door while she was alone in the house. When her sister came home and asked if she was okay, relief had washed over her in waves. She didn't tell Claire everything that had happened. She thought maybe it had been partly her fault. Of course, if she had, Claire would have told her it wasn't. But she didn't; she was just glad to have someone to talk to and spend the evening with.

Claire didn't push Theresa for an explanation. She could see she was upset, and she wanted to help. Her little sister was an independent soul, a free spirit who had always been determined to do things her own way. If she pushed her for an explanation, she knew that she would end up further away from an answer than ever. So she did what she could, which was make some strawberry milkshakes and sit and watch telly with Theresa, telling her about her day and talking about how excited and nervous she was about leaving for university.

When this appeared to make her even more unhappy, she changed the subject again. Her revelation about getting a copy of The Modern Lovers album seemed to do the trick. Theresa had insisted that they go upstairs and listen to it straight away, leading to an evening of record listening in Claire's room, which seemed to take Theresa's mind off of whatever it was that was bothering her.

THIRTEEN

I didn't see Bert the following day or the day after that. My Nan made an unannounced visit, pulling up outside the house in the enormous blue Rover that had been my grandfather's sole domain until he died a couple of years ago. Since then, Nan had taken the wheel, relishing her independence and adding some dents and scratches that would have made Grandad turn in his grave if he hadn't been cremated.

Nan was ancient. Despite the heat, she would never be seen out without her cardigan and was perpetually shrouded in a fug of smoke and rose water. Her greeting to me was to tell me how big I'd grown, although it was only Easter when we last visited her. I'm pretty sure I hadn't grown that much since then. Then she asked me to be a dear and collect her luggage from the car, a huge leather suitcase with her initials embossed on it, alongside several faded stickers from what seemed to me impossibly exotic locations: Spain, St Moritz, Geneva. I think my grandparents managed an adventure or two.

As always, she took over the house, dominating the kitchen and arranging a full rota of activities for all of us. Dad kind of stayed out of the way, even though her visit was ostensibly 'to check he was okay after his scare.' Mum surrendered to the inevitable but made sure she kept me nearby for moral support.

I bounced around on the enormous back seat of the car when we went out for a picnic, which ended prematurely when it turned out it was too hot for Nan. Who would have guessed that it was going to be hot again today? It's not as if they talked about anything else on the radio or that it hadn't been scorching hot every other day this month – or last. I ate the sweets she produced from her handbag at regular intervals and helped her to find things that she had put down – glasses, car keys, cigarette lighter, purse, a glass of port. You name it, if it could be mislaid, Nan would.

I hoped I might get to have my campout while she stayed, as she usually slept in my room. Instead, I was bundled onto the sofa, where I slept under a spare sheet after everyone else had gone to bed for the night. I was woken up when the first riser (usually Nan) got up for their morning cup of tea.

Once I was awake, Nan would give me fifty pence from her purse and ask me to go and get her a packet of Dunhill from the newsagents. We both knew I wasn't supposed to, but she had given the shop owner such a hard time on her previous visit that I don't think he dared to refuse me when I turned up with a note from Nan and told him she was staying again. With Nan, I was allowed to keep the change; it was only a few pence, but the handful of blackjacks and fruit salads made the trip worthwhile.

My memories of Nan, when I was younger before Grandad died, were of a quiet lady who spent most of her time making sure that Grandad had everything he needed. Now it was different, Mum said that Nan was 'living her best life', and she certainly seemed to be to me. When Mum said it, she didn't necessarily make it sound like a good thing, although she never said as much. They would both refer to Grandad regularly, deciding which things he would and wouldn't have liked and reminding one another of some of the things he did and said. Neither of them appeared to recall how he would boss everybody about and insist on having everything his own way all the time.

When it was time for Nan to leave, she had managed to round up all her possessions and had me carry her suitcase back out to the car and heave it up into the boot. She took me to one side and showed me four fifty pence pieces, which she pressed into my hand,

"Don't tell your mum, get yourself something." She leaned over and kissed me on the cheek with her hairy chin brushing against me, then started to climb into her car and put on her driving gloves.

I was beyond excited at this sudden and unexpected windfall, I slipped the coins into my pocket and waved Nan off while I was planning how I would spend it.

***

The following morning, I finished walking the dog, along with the minimal chores that had been left for me, then went straight round to Bert's. He answered the door and looked down at my towel in my hand,

"Hi, Shorts, are we off to the beach?" He went back inside to collect his trunks, I followed him in and got his attention by rattling the money in my hand.

"Oh, cool, where did you get that?"

"My Nan came to stay. You know what it means, don't you?"

Bert looked blankly at me.

"It means we can go to the lido; I'll pay for you to get in."

"Are you sure? It's your money."

"I'm sure. Get your stuff."

The lido was a large open-air swimming pool on the seafront. Usually, I didn't have the funds to go there, but today, I did, and I intended to get there early and make the most of it. The deal with the lido was that once you had paid to go in, you could stay as long as you wanted, which was exactly what the kids did. The only catch was that you couldn't go out and then come back, which didn't worry me as I was planning on staying for the day.

Once me and Bert were through the old metal turnstile, we looked around to see who else was about. Several boys from our year at school had claimed a space down near the shallow end. There was a strict hierarchy for the seating; sets of concrete terraces lined one side of the pool, the younger kids got to sit at the shallow end. It graduated after that; the older you were, the closer to the deep end you could set up camp. I had never actually seen this rule being enforced, but rumour had it that the big kids would throw your stuff in the pool if you encroached on their territory.

It was kind of nice to catch up with some of the other kids and find out what they had all been doing this summer. Some had been away in tents and caravans with their families and were glad to be back. Others were still to go and were looking forward to it. Some, like me and Bert, had just been hanging around at home while their parents worked. Everyone agreed that it was good being off school, even if there wasn't that much to do. The exception to this was 'Speccy' Brown, who told us all he was looking forward to going back. We all took the Mickey, of course, with regular comments resurfacing about how things were not as much fun as school – all directed at Speccy, who played along with the teasing in good humour.

The lido was loud and busy from the outset that day, with kids competing for who could make the biggest splash when they bombed, families with younger children vying for space, and the bigger boys trying to impress the girls - who mostly ignored them as they spread themselves on their towels in the sun. Occasionally, the lifeguard would blow his whistle for some misdemeanour or other, although nobody seemed to take much notice, kids would just wait until he wasn't looking to take an illicit run-up for their turn at bombing.

The absence of Alan and Tubs was a relief and a blessing. Bert had assured me that his brother was skint and they weren't likely to show up. I asked if he'd seen Theresa and Janet over the last few days, but he seemed a bit vague, unsure of whether they'd been to the house or not. I looked over at the area where the older kids sat in the hope that I might see Theresa there, but she wasn't.

The complete and utter absence of any shaded area in the morning meant that a lot of time was spent in the water cooling off. After midday, there was some respite from the heat if you were close to the wall, although most of the kids didn't seem that bothered. There had already been enough sun that summer to ensure that everybody had a deep brown tan. Blisters and peeling skin had now faded to make way for freckles and bronzed limbs and bodies.

By mid-afternoon, I was feeling hot and hungry. I wished I had thought to bring something to eat, but it was too late now. As we climbed out of the pool side-by-side, I asked Bert if he had had enough.

"Yeah, I'm getting too hot."

"Do you want to get some chips?"

It was a rhetorical question, I didn't wait for an answer but started to dress as Bert did the same.

Before long, we were sat on the sea wall, a bundle of newspaper wrapped around some chips, smothered in salt and vinegar, on our laps. We shared our food and watched the people who crowded the sand, and I thought life might not get any better than this.

FOURTEEN

As I had managed to avoid Tubs for a few days, I started to relax a bit, thinking he may have forgotten about me for now and moved on to tormenting someone else. It turned out that I was wrong about that, but for now, I enjoyed the respite. Bert saw Alan regularly, of course, but from what I could gather, they rarely spoke to one another, and the flimsy peace deal was still holding in their house.

After walking to the newsagent to spend some more of what was left of Nan's money on two ice poles, we walked back, squeezing the last of the melted juice from the plastic wrapper.

"Shall we go up there?" asked Bert.

I looked up to where he was pointing, the disused viaduct that towered over the top end of the town. It used to bring goods trains into the station from along the coast, but now one end had been demolished, meaning it stopped abruptly long before it got there. In the other direction, you could follow the abandoned cuttings to the very top end of town and beyond.

"We're not supposed to," I answered.

"So?" replied Bert with a shrug, he led me to the fenced-off end, where large signs informed us that it was *'strictly forbidden to access this area'* and that it was an *'unsafe structure – do not enter.'* Bert went directly to a small gate set into the security fence that blocked access to the area. The sturdy padlock looked intimidating, so I was surprised when Bert simply pulled it towards him on its rusty hinges. The huge hasp was not joined to the frame anymore, presumably pulled away by a previous generation of kids. He held the gate open while assuring me that,

"Nobody ever checks, who's going to know?"

I suspected that Mum would know somehow. Nevertheless, I went through the gate behind him. Together, we walked the short distance to look over the edge of the crumbling brick parapet. I felt a familiar wave of nausea as Bert walked right to the edge of the precipice, standing precariously on the jagged end, and then sat himself down with his legs dangling over the edge. Slowly, I followed him, inching towards the brink until I finally joined him on his perch. Despite my misgivings, the brickwork did not crumble and collapse underneath us.

The view was magnificent, a full panorama of the town spreading out in every direction, from the shops to the beach to the estuary and the ocean. I was mesmerised as I watched the people crawling like ants on the pavements while toy cars navigated the 3D map below us. We sat and pointed out the various landmarks to each other: the school, the distant clock tower, and various shops. But most of all, we studied the aerial view of the Wilds. From our vantage point, we could make out all the paths and tracks that were almost invisible at ground level. The Grotty Grotto was not quite in the centre but offset towards the town. The area of bushes between it and the train track was dense and mostly unbroken, spreading most of the way towards the station. There was nobody there today, and tiny movements gave clues as to the location of the rabbits that lived somewhere in this fenced-in jungle.

I don't know how long we stayed up on our castle, it felt like forever. Eventually, we walked back along the compacted gravel that had once formed a base for the train tracks, now long gone. We went back through the gate, and I continued to follow the old tracks along to the point where the embankment started to level off to rejoin the pavement.

"This way's quicker," Bert pointed at the steep bank to our left.

I looked dubiously at the near vertical slope. The sparse vegetation was interspersed with bare lines of earth where rainwater had run off, creating miniature rivers and waterfalls that washed everything in its path away. Having seen no rain for months, they were now trails of dry and dusty mud.

I was about to question the wisdom of this suggestion, but Bert was already stepping forward, putting one foot on the bank and shifting his weight from his back foot. He immediately shot forward, the loose top surface billowing up in a cloud of dust as Bert fell on his backside and vanished from view. I rushed to the edge and looked down, half expecting to see Bert in a bloody heap of tangled and broken limbs. Instead, I saw him clambering to his feet at the bottom of the incline. He was brushing the layer of red dust that had coated him, pulling a twig from his hair and laughing.

"Come on down, Shorts, it's brilliant!"

It didn't look brilliant, it looked terrifying. Below me, Bert dashed into a nearby bush and reappeared, holding two grubby plastic bags, he ran around to the lower end of the slope and then back along to me, handing me one of the bags.

"What's this for?" I asked. He didn't answer, he put his bag on the lip of the slope, sat on it and promptly disappeared again, this time with a protracted shout of joy as he descended.

I tentatively placed my bag on the ground, lowering myself into position and then sitting on it. I slowly, cautiously edged my way towards the incline. There was a brief moment when I could have possibly stopped myself and taken the path instead. I hesitated for a fraction of a second – then I flew.

It was far from a smooth ride, every bump, stone and imperfection jolted through me as I hurtled downwards in my own flurry of red dust and dried mud. I came to an abrupt halt at the bottom, rolling onto my side on the edge of the grass. Bert's face loomed over me, a smile on his dirt-streaked face, and we both started to laugh.

"Fantastic, let's go again."

Bert didn't need to be asked twice, we raced back to the top and repeated the process. We did this several more times. Our descents offered no opportunity for control or finesse; it was pure speed, adrenaline, hope and luck. We stood and looked at one another, literally plastered in a thick coat of dust from head to toe.

"My Mum's going to kill me," I said as I tried to brush myself clean.

"Come back to mine, we'll get cleaned up a bit before you go home, It'll be fine."

Bert seemed quietly confident about this, but I could feel a hole in the seat of my shorts, and the dirt was pretty well ground in, I wasn't as certain. Nevertheless, we went back to Bert's house to try and remove at least the worst of the mess.

Traipsing powdered mud through the hall and kitchen, we went into the back garden. Mum would have had a fit if we'd done that in my house, I guess his mum didn't mind as much as mine. Here, Bert attempted, ineffectually, to clean me up with the head of the broom. I reciprocated, with the same lack of success, and was starting to resign myself to whatever reprimands were going to come my way. I could already hear Mum's voice in my head,

'What on earth have you been doing? How did you get into such a state? Wait 'till your father gets home.'

But Bert had another plan up his sleeve, he pulled a length of hosepipe out from beside the shed and started to attach it to the garden tap.

"You can't do that," I informed him, "there's a hosepipe ban."

"It's okay because we're not watering the garden, are we?" Bert replied as he turned on the tap and held the hose over his head. The logic of the argument seemed sound to me, I watched as Bert gasped under the onslaught of the jet of water that poured over him, returning his hair to its normal colour. In turn, his face lost its resemblance to one of the black and white minstrels that Mum liked watching on telly, his clothes became drenched and a pool of brown water started to gather at his feet. Satisfied, he passed the hose to me and I got to experience first-hand just how cold the water was.

After some splashing and laughing we eventually turned the water off and stood dripping in the sunshine as the sun started to gradually warm us up again. Our wet clothes stuck to our skinny bodies and we stood looking at our newly cleaned selves as we decided what to do next, we appeared to have swapped one problem for another. Peeling off our wet tee shirts, we laid them out on the grass to dry in the sun, putting our shoes and shorts next to them. My underpants were wet too, but there was no way I was taking them off. Bert went inside and returned moments later with two towels that we wrapped around ourselves, draping them over our shoulders while the sun did its work.

It's quite boring watching things dry, so we retreated to the shade of the house where we settled in Bert's room – after first confirming that there was nothing of interest on any of the three TV channels. We were sitting on the bed listening to music, talking and laughing as we recounted the wild, muddy slides of the morning with our towels draped around ourselves like ponchos. I'm not sure why Bert decided not to put on some dry clothes, I guess it was just too hot.

Downstairs the front door banged open and was then slammed shut as three sets of footsteps clattered up the stairs. Alan and Tubs' voices argued about some unidentified misdeed and whose fault something had been. The third voice, when we heard it, I recognised as Janet's. Alan's bedroom door opened then closed and muffled music started to thump through the partition wall. I breathed a sigh of relief, happy to have avoided another encounter with Tubs.

"We can go over to my house if you want, for a change," I suggested. I didn't need to explain, I knew Bert understood.

"Yeah, okay," he answered, "we'll go in a minute. I'll just finish reading this first."

We were both reading comics. We'd swapped some the previous week. It seemed reasonable, and I carried on thumbing through a funny old black and white Eagle annual where Dan Dare was fighting the Mekons.

The music from next door suddenly increased in volume as the door opened, Alan's voice rose above the racket,

"Just fuck off for five minutes, give us a bit of privacy."

"What'll I do?"

"I dunno, watch the fucking telly or something."

The door shut firmly, and Tubs stomped downstairs, muttering audibly about what a fucking twat Alan was. The TV went on, changed channels a few times then was switched off again. The kitchen tap ran, and the fridge opened and closed. From next door, there was giggling and mumbling from under the cacophony of the music. Downstairs was quiet for a moment, and then Tubs started to stomp back up the stairs. I had just had time to think how mad Alan would be; Tubs had only been gone for a minute or two. Then Bert's bedroom door swung slowly open to reveal Tubs standing, grinning, in the doorway. He stepped forward into the room, and his grin became a leer as he started to speak,

"Look at you two, all snuggled up nude together. I know what you've been up to."

"Get lost, Tubs," Bert responded, apparently confident that this would send him on his way. It didn't. Faster than you would suspect was possible for someone so ungainly, Tubs was across the room and looming over us. His shirt had the legend 'save water – drink beer' printed on it in stretched-taught letters, there was an orange stain on his left shoulder that spread down to his belly in streaks and spots. It was matched by a cracked smear of food sticking to the side of his mouth.

"Shut your mouth, or I'll smash your teeth in," he snarled. His face had contorted into an ugly mask of hatred, his raised voice carrying to us on a current of fetid breath. Terrified after my last run-in with Tubs, I just wanted whatever was going to happen to be over, Bert, however, was not yet ready to give in. He started to stand up and was immediately pushed back onto the bed, where Tubs grabbed a handful of his long black hair and twisted it tightly around his fist.

"You're going to stay right here, nancy boy, I know what you and your little boyfriend have been up to in here, poofs."

Bert started to speak, but his hair was twisted more forcefully, and he stopped abruptly. I stared at the stain on Tubs' shirt, in the moment, I found myself trying to decide if it was bean juice. Tubs was not finished.

"I'm fucking bored of waiting for your brother to finish fingering his slag girlfriend, it's your fault I haven't got anything to have a go on myself."

I realised he was looking directly at me now, I had no idea what he was talking about and just stared back at him, open-mouthed and confused.

"Don't pretend you don't know," his voice now was low and ominous, "you've been chatting her up and getting her presents. She was meant to be my girlfriend, that's why Janet bought her with her."

I was starting to understand what Tubs was talking about, but I hadn't been chatting up Theresa – had I? She was one of the big girls. I kind of liked her, but I never imagined for a minute that she would think of me as anything other than a kid. I wanted to explain this to Tubs but found that not only was I too afraid to speak, but that I didn't have the words to express what I was thinking even if I could. My mouth opened and closed soundlessly as I looked at the stain. It was irrelevant, Tubs had already worked himself up to the point that he wouldn't have listened anyway. He looked at me, and I averted my eyes from his, pulling my eyes away from the remains of his breakfast – or tea, or whichever meal it was, on his mouth and shirt. My ears buzzed, and I was finding it hard to follow what he was saying. Suddenly, his hand flicked out and slapped across my cheek. Bert wriggled but was pinned down, and I suddenly became fully focused again.

"I said she wouldn't fancy you so much if she knew you were a bender, would she?"

"But I'm not," I answered, earning myself another slap that I mostly – but not entirely, dodged this time.

"We'll see, shall we? Kiss him." He yanked back on Bert's hair and pushed his face towards mine, tilted upwards. If the expression on Tubs' face was malevolent, Bert's was pure hatred. He wriggled and tried to turn away but was held fast in Tubs' grip. As I looked at Bert, a sudden pain stung across my cheek as Tubs lashed out at me again.

"Fucking do it, bum boy, or next time I'll bash your teeth down your throat."

I looked at the now bunched-up fist, then back at Bert, unsure of what to do next. I was positive that Tubs would carry through on his threat, and I was scared. Bert looked me in the eye and, as best he could, gave a small nod of his head. I leaned forward and then, at the last moment, darted my head towards him and gave him a peck on the cheek, like the one Nan had given me when she left. This seemed to infuriate Tubs even more,

"Not like that, twat. A proper kiss on the lips, do it – now!"

Scared, I moved towards Bert again and offered the same brief touch as before, but this time to his lips. As our mouths made contact, Tubs' hand grasped the back of my neck, pinching it with force and pushing my head forward. Our lips mashed up against each other's, and I silently wondered how much longer this was going to go on, I closed my eyes and waited for it to finish.

When it came, the end was quick. Laughing loudly, Tubs released his hold on both of us and then, just as we started to pull apart, hit us both on the back of our respective heads. Our faces clashed, my cheek bashing against Bert's, our lips and teeth forced together again in a rush, and I tasted blood in my mouth.

Then it was over, Tubs stood back and grinned at us,

"See, I knew you were a pair of fairies."

He walked out laughing. We sat frozen as he clattered back down the stars, and the TV was switched back on.

The blood I had tasted was not mine. I could see Bert's lower lip was swollen, and from the side of his mouth, a thin red trail ran down to his chin and dripped onto his bare chest. I wiped my mouth, first with the back of my hand, then with the towel. Bert did the same – only more gingerly. He had tears in his eyes, and I suppose I did too. But Bert's were not like mine; I was aching from the indignity and humiliation of what had happened. My feelings of helplessness and the inability to fight back overcame my emotions. Not Bert's, it was plain to see from his rigid expression and clenched teeth that his tears were born of fury.

"I'm going to fucking kill him," he growled in a low menacing voice. It scared me a little, Bert was usually so chilled, one of life's happy souls. Right now, he looked like anger personified. I reached out with my hand and put it on his arm,

"It's okay, it's done now," I told him.

He flinched slightly as my hand touched his bare skin. He looked down at it, then surprised me as he took it in his trembling hand. He seemed to be calming a little; the tears had stopped, and the expression on his face was less severe than it had been a moment ago. Downstairs, Tubs was still in the sitting room, the TV blaring and the music from next door continued unabated.

"It's not, he'll keep coming back. He's a bully, and we need to do something about it."

I thought about telling Mum, but I didn't think I'd be able to. The last thing I wanted was to get in trouble with her and not be allowed around Bert's again. I didn't think Bert's mum would do anything either. I was mulling over what we could do when another thought occurred to me,

"Do you think we are poofs?"

"Eh? What do you mean?" Bert was pulling a pair of jeans and a tee shirt from his drawer and putting them on.

"I mean, what if we're homos?"

I had little or no idea of what that meant. Generally, they were words we used to taunt or tease other lads. Usually in a good-humoured way, although not always. I had the vaguest idea that it was about sex between men but didn't even really understand how sex between men and women worked yet, so it was outside my comprehension. Bert seemed to have a better idea than me,

"Do you like girls?"

I pulled a bit of face, and then I thought of Theresa. I remembered how much I had enjoyed sitting and talking to her, the feeling of being close to her and how I looked forward to seeing her again. I answered,

"Yes, I suppose."

"Did you want to kiss me?"

"No."

"Well, you're probably not a queer then, don't worry about it."

It never occurred to me to ask Bert the same questions: why would it? I was happy to have had my worries put to rest, or at least as happy as I could be given the recent events.

Bert reached for some dry shoes from under his bed; he carried them to the door before looking out to check that the coast was clear. We snuck quietly down the stairs and into the garden to retrieve my clothes. The sides that had been facing the sun were now warm and dry. Underneath, they were still damp and clammy. When I put them on, I thought they looked less dirty than they had earlier, I was hopeful that I might get away with it when I got home. We slipped out of the front door, past the sitting room where we could hear Tubs chuckling along to a kid's show, and walked back towards my house.

Aside from the background noises of cars, insects and a distant ice cream van, it was a quiet walk. I suppose neither of us was sure where to start. As we neared home, Bert broke our silence,

"Sorry."

"Sorry, what?"

"Sorry about what happened, you know…."

I did know, but I didn't think it was Bert's fault. I wasn't sure what I was going to say until I blurted out,

"Tubs is a bloody bastard. I hate his guts."

"Yeah, me too. I'm going to get him back."

I looked at Bert and saw that he had every intention of getting retribution, but I had no idea how,

"How? He's bigger than us."

Bert gently touched his swollen lip and considered it; I think it was the most serious I had ever seen him look.

"I'll think of something. We're going to get him Shorts. We'll bloody get the fat cunt."

I made a mental note that the revenge plan had now been extended to include me, which wasn't surprising. But I was still dubious that we would be able to do anything. We arrived at my front path.

"Coming in?"

"Nah, I'm going for a walk. I'll see you tomorrow, yeah?"

"Okay, come round. See you."

I watched Bert as he carried on up the road, going to wherever it was he went on his walks when home was not an option. Another mystery that, with the benefit of time and hindsight, maybe I could and should have asked more about.

I went around the side of the house with the intention of slipping in quietly and unnoticed via the kitchen. I was, of course, wrong about that. Kisses for Me was playing on the radio, and Mum and Auntie Jean were sitting at the table talking, with steaming mugs of coffee in front of them. The table is big, with six chairs placed around it. I'm not sure why because we never have more than four people at a time in our house. I stopped dead and was puzzled over why they would have hot drinks on a boiling day like this when Mum looked in my direction.

"Look at the state of you, what on earth have you been up to? No, actually, don't tell me, I don't want to know."

This answered the question of whether I had managed to get the worst of the grime off my clothes. I was also relieved that I wasn't going to have to explain myself, I knew for a certainty that if I started to tell one part of the story, I would end up telling it all. Probably bursting into tears in front of Auntie Jean into the bargain.

Auntie Jean smiled at me, took a sip of her coffee, then tutted and shook her head,

"Boys, what are they like, eh?"

Mum didn't answer, she was on her feet now and inspecting me from a range of different angles.

"I don't think you could have got any dirtier if you'd tried, and you've ripped your shorts. Go up now and run a bath before you get mud all over the house."

My tee shirt was being pulled up over my head; Mum paused to hold her thumb and forefinger a short distance apart,

"This deep, there's a water shortage, and make sure you scoop the water out into the buckets when you're done. The flowers need it."

Three mismatched plastic buckets had been repurposed from the garden and had taken up residence in the bathroom, used bathwater had to be decanted into them so they could be taken out and tipped onto the flower beds. I thought the flowers, already wilted and dried out, were a lost cause – but Mum still insisted.

"Yes, Mum," I answered as I kicked my shoes off and ran up the stairs.

I was quite surprised by the amount of red silt and grit that was left in the bottom of the bath when I was finished, I carefully carried the buckets downstairs one at a time and poured them onto the plants before being presented with a plate of fish fingers and fried eggs. I was allowed to take them to my room as Mum and Auntie Jean were still deep in conversation.

That night, I dreamed I was on the beach with Bert, In the dream, he leaned over and kissed me. Not the violent coupling inflicted by Tubs that afternoon, but a proper kiss, like James Bond in the various films that I had managed to pester Dad into letting me watch all or part of. I awoke in the darkness to discover that my pyjama trousers were wet. This had happened before, leading to an excruciating conversation with Mum, after which she had presented me with a small booklet about puberty. It was slightly old-fashioned and medical, but I knew what wet dreams were now.

I changed into a pair of pants and threw my pyjama trousers towards the door with the rest of my dirty clothes from the day. They hadn't quite made it to the basket on the landing yet. Back in bed, covered by a single sheet, I tried to get back to sleep. I tossed and turned in the humid heat of the night, listening as the distant sound of the church clock striking, first once, then twice, drifted in through the open window. My head was crowded with thoughts and questions: Did I like girls? – I was pretty sure I did. Did I want to kiss Bert? –

no, Tubs had made me. Was I queer? – probably not, the dream didn't mean anything at all. Was I confused? – definitely.

Deep, dreamless sleep caught up with me eventually, the earlier dream and the unanswered questions were all left behind for another night.

FIFTEEN

The following morning, Bert was back to his usual enthusiastic self. He let himself in through the side gate and found me in the back garden after failing to get an answer when he knocked at the front door. He came and sat on the step next to me, and we took turns throwing Max's slobbery ball to the end of the garden, from where it was collected and dropped back at our feet.

"Did you catch it last night?" I asked, "My Mum was mad when I got in."

"Nah, I didn't go back 'till after Tubs had pissed off. Mum was watching TV by then. She didn't even notice." He said this in a blasé way, but I thought I detected something else in his voice like maybe he wished someone had noticed.

"What're we going to do about Tubs?" he asked.

"Stay out of his way?"

"That's easy for you to say, he doesn't keep coming round your house."

That was true. I had no adequate response to this, so I just looked up at the bright disc of the sun in the blue sky and made myself squint. The ball dropped at my feet, and I picked it up and threw it into the bushes, where it would take Max longer to find it again.

"He's too big for us to beat up, even both of us together," I said, "I don't know anyone who would help us either."

There was a long, quiet pause as we both sat in silent contemplation. Max left his ball and came and sat with us as if he, too, was trying to work out what we could do. Bert sat up straight and looked at me,

"I know someone who might help us. Not to beat him up, but to keep him out of the way."

"Who?"

"Your friend Theresa."

"She's not really my friend," I blushed, "I don't know her that well."

"No, but she likes you for some stupid reason that I can't work out."

"Likes me?"

"Yeah, she keeps talking to you and making you tapes. It's why Tubs is so mad with you. He fancies the pants off her."

I didn't know how to respond to this. I knew that I liked her, but it had never occurred to me that she might have any opinion about me. Now Bert said it, it made sense.

"Why would she help us? Her and Janet are friends with Tubs and Alan."

"Not from what I heard last night. Alan was talking to Janet on the phone. I didn't get exactly what it was, but I got some of it, they're both mad with Tubs – he did something to upset Theresa the other day, and Janet doesn't like Tubs hanging around with them all the time."

"What did he do?"

"I don't know, but if she's pissed off with him, she might agree to help us get our own back."

"I don't know…" It felt a bit like we would be using her, probably because we would be. I still couldn't guess what the plan might be. But if Bert was right, if she was cross with him, she might not mind too much. I was curious as to what revenge Bert was plotting; I just hoped that it wasn't something that would make things worse.

"So, what are we going to do then?"

Bert explained what he was thinking to me. It was simpler than digging pits and putting wooden spikes in the bottom, but it all hinged on whether Theresa would agree to play her part in it.

"So that's where you come in," he said excitedly, "you take back one of the tapes you borrowed and then see if you can work it into the conversation."

I wasn't sure about the plan, any of it, in particular, Bert's certainty that I would be able to persuade Theresa to help us. But he had complete faith in his idea, his belief in it was absolute. There had been a certainty in his voice when he had outlined his plan that left no room for doubt.

"Well," I said, "we can't do that until I see Theresa again."

A withering look from Bert told me that he wasn't going to wait.

"We can go to her house, call for her."

Of course, Bert knew where Theresa lived; he seemed to know where everyone's house was. I looked over at Max, who had now slunk over to lie in the shade beside the shed, it was too hot even for him.

"We can take my stinky dog, Theresa seemed to like him. Shall we do it tomorrow?"

"No Shorts, we need to do it now – while the plan's still fresh in our minds."

I agreed, although a bit reluctantly. I wasn't sure I wanted to rush into anything, but Bert was insistent. We retreated inside to fine-tune the details of the plan and have a drink of squash before going back out into the heat of the day – the slightly mad dog and the English boys.

I found some spare bits of paper (I say 'found'; they were the middle pages torn out of one of my school books that currently sat redundant and forgotten on the bedroom floor), and we made notes so we didn't forget what we needed to say to Theresa. I picked up the tape with Transformer on, we collected a slightly refreshed Max from the garden, and we went to put Bert's plan into action.

Although maybe I shouldn't call it that any more, it was my plan too now - I was a co-conspirator.

SIXTEEN

It was steep, and it felt like the hill would go on forever as I plodded upwards past the rows of red brick terraced houses with sweat dripping down my back. We had walked through the park, where Max went a bit bonkers - like he always does. He loves it when we go to open spaces dotted with trees and things to sniff. Now, Bert was leading us upwards through a maze of back roads towards our destination.

The pavement felt like it had a kind of spongey quality to it, I wouldn't say the tarmac was melting - but it was definitely feeling softer under my plimsolls. I had heard on the radio that train tracks had been buckling in the heat. On the news, they had said that some roads had started to crumble as the relentless onslaught of the weather started to break up the surface. Even if it was all in my head, the thought of my feet sinking into the ground each time I pushed myself a little further up the hill did not make it easier. Max kept himself to whichever side of me offered the shade of a low garden wall as he panted along with his tongue lolling out the side of his open mouth.

Finally, Bert came to a halt. He pointed to a large house with a well-tended but as dry as all the others, garden at the front and a blue front door. I still didn't know how he knew it was her house, but he had no trace of uncertainty, so naturally, I believed him.

"What now?" I asked.

"We go and knock on the door, see if she's in."

After the trek we had just undertaken, I hoped she was, I didn't want to have to come back again later. There was also a part of me that sort of hoped she wasn't. A sense of nervous anticipation engulfed me – and maybe a bit of shyness. It made no difference, Bert had already opened the gate and was on his way up the path. I hurried to follow him, catching up just as he pressed the doorbell. We waited, I was just about to give up when I heard footsteps from inside the house. They approached the door, and it was pulled open. In front of us stood Theresa, only it wasn't, it was an older, more grown-up version of her – what she might look like in five or six years.

"Hello?" said not Theresa.

"Is Theresa in?" asked Bert, unphased.

"She's in the garden, go round the side gate. Is that your dog? He's cute."

"Thanks," I mumbled, it seemed like it had been a good idea to drag Max along after all. I trailed behind Bert as he followed the directions to the side of the house.

Theresa did not seem in the least surprised to see us, she got off her sun lounger and came to greet us in her yellow bikini. As she bent down to fuss over Max, I didn't know where to look, or at least I did, but it didn't feel right, so I averted my eyes.

"Hello, Max," she stroked and patted him, and he sniffed around her legs excitedly. "Are you thirsty? Do you want some water? You must be boiling in that furry coat." She looked at us, "Do you want a drink, there's some squash in the fridge, I'll go and get it."

Soon, we were all sat on the scrubby, yellow grass with glasses of squash, apart from Max, who had lapped up a saucepan full of water before he sniffed his way around the garden. He was now resting in the shade at the side of the house with his second pan of water nearby. I was starting to find it a little easier to be in the company of a nearly naked girl, Bert seemed to be completely unaffected as he sipped his cold drink and ran the cool glass across his forehead, leaving a trail of condensation in its wake.

"Well, it's nice to see you, were you just passing, or is this a special visit?" there was a slight smile on her face as she asked this as if she might have guessed that we had an ulterior motive for visiting. I produced the tape from my pocket'

"I was bringing this back."

"Well, thanks," she took it off me and put it on the grass next to her drink, "I've got some more for you upstairs, I'll go and get them in a minute. My sister, Claire, the one who answered the door, works at Smiths on the record counter. She gets all sorts of good things. I've put some Velvet Underground on a tape for you, that's Lou Reed's first band. You'll love it."

"Thanks, I remember you telling me about them, I'll look forward to it." This was partially true, I remembered now she said it, but if you'd asked me to name Lou Reed's first band ten minutes ago, I wouldn't have been able to tell you to save my life.

"We have another reason for coming as well, actually," Bert blurted out, unable to contain himself, "we need your help."

"Well, now I'm intrigued, what wicked plan could you possibly need my assistance for?"

Bert told Theresa about the bullying and beatings we had been suffering at the hands of Tubs. She didn't seem overly surprised, although her expression changed dramatically from its previous smile as the story unfolded. Bert stopped short of telling her everything. I was glad, I didn't want anyone – especially not Theresa - to know about the kiss.

"Did he do that to you?" she pointed to his still-swollen lip.

"Yes."

"So, how do you want me to help? He won't stop just because I ask him to. I'm not even speaking to him anymore."

"You don't have to talk to him, just write him a note. Tell him to meet you in the Wilds, then make him sit and wait in the hot sun. He'll wait for ages if he thinks you're coming, he'll sit in the heat of the day. He'll be really pissed off by the time he realises nobody's coming."

"Yeah, with me. Why couldn't you just write the note?"

I looked at Bert, neither of us had thought of that. I took the piece of paper out of my pocket and looked at what we had written, Theresa leaned over and took it off me. She read it, then laughed.

"Okay, I see why you need me to help now." She held the piece of paper up, "This is real boy writing; it couldn't be any harder to read if you'd written it in French, and I imagine Tubs has a hard job reading at the best of times." She grinned, showing off that wonky eye tooth that only made everything else look more perfect, and passed the paper back to me. "I'll do it, but I'm not signing it, if he ever asks if it was me, I'll just deny it. What if he finds out you two were behind it, though?"

Again, it was not something we had even considered. It was turning out we were not the criminal masterminds we had thought we were.

"Why would he?" asked Bert. "It's only a joke, something to get back at him a bit."

"Well, let me go and get some paper, and I'll write it for you. I'll even correct your spelling if you want. How are you going to know if he falls for it?"

"We're going to watch from the top of the bunker. He won't see us, but we'll see him."

"Then you'll get sunburn too, won't you?"

"It'll be worth it," Bert asserted, "anyway, we don't have to stay the whole time, do we?"

"I suppose not, hold on here then."

I watched Theresa walk into the house, her backside barely contained by the stretched-thin yellow fabric of her bikini bottom until Bert punched my arm.

"Oi, put your eyes back in their sockets. You fancy her, don't you?"

I blushed and denied it, but now Bert had said it again, and we both knew it was true. We finished our drinks while we waited for Theresa to come back. When she did, she had a tape and a pale pink envelope in her hand. She passed one to me and the other to Bert.

"I told him to be there at two o'clock tomorrow afternoon, he'll probably get there early, so he'll be plenty hot enough by the time he realises nobody's coming," she smiled. I don't know if I read something into that smile that wasn't there, but it seemed like Theresa had her reasons for wanting to help with this.

Bert smiled and held the envelope in his hand,

"Thanks, Theresa, we'll let you know how long he stays – unless you want to come and watch with us."

I hoped she would say yes, I would have liked it if she had agreed to spend the afternoon with us. But she declined, telling us she would leave us to our revenge and to enjoy it. We collected Max and started the long walk back down the hill.

I'm not sure why, but I had assumed we were going home now. Another glaring omission in my planning. Luckily, Bert had it covered,

"Shorts, this way."

I turned to see he had stopped at the end of a cut-through. He led me down the narrow alley, heading towards the housing estate at the top end of town.

"Where are we going?"

"To deliver this to Tubs." He waved the envelope in front of me.

"But we don't know where he lives."

"You don't, I do, come on," he carried on walking past the waist-high weeds that crowded the edge of the path, with me and Max following.

Eventually, we arrived outside a house with a broken gate wedged up on a brick, the faded blue paint peeling off in strips. The front garden was bare, not because it was parched and dying like the others, but because nothing had been growing there in the first place. There was a broken kids' bike in the overgrown hedge and a stained mattress in the middle of the space that would have been the lawn on any other house. The sound of a radio drifted out from an open upstairs window – encouraging whoever was singing along with it to 'Shake Shake Shake - Shake your Booty', so someone was definitely in. Even though it was a female voice, I was scared that Tubs would appear and catch us delivering the letter.

"What if he sees us?" I whispered.

"He won't. He was going out with Alan this afternoon; he'll be long gone."

Nevertheless, neither of us was keen to approach the house and post it through the letterbox. Bert took a deep breath and then walked briskly up the path in what he thought was a casual manner, although it wasn't really, he looked stilted and awkward.

He stopped dead in his tracks when a voice boomed out from inside the house,

"What the fuck are you doing?"

The singing stopped abruptly, and a second voice shouted back,

"I'm fucking getting ready to go out."

"Well, turn that shit music down, I'm trying to watch telly."

I let out the breath that I didn't realise I had been holding when I realised that both voices were female. Tubs' big sisters, I knew them by reputation and didn't fancy a face-to-face meeting with either of them – let alone the two of them together. I silently urged Bert to carry on.

He dashed to the door, posted the letter, and then almost ran back to me. Together, we left the scene of the crime as quickly as we could without running, only stopping when not only the house but the entire road was out of sight.

Once we had put some distance between ourselves and Tub's house, we slowed down to a steady walking pace, stopping when we reached a wall that was a convenient height to sit on and catch our breath. Bert started to laugh.

"What's funny?" I asked.

"That was hairy," was his reply.

"But…I thought you said he wouldn't be home."

"I don't think he was, but his sisters were."

"Yeah, but nobody saw us – did they?"

"I don't think so."

I supposed that would have to be good enough for now. I changed the subject,

"Do you think he'll show up?"

"I don't know, what did Theresa put in the letter?"

"I don't know, it was stuck down."

I realised, again, that there were big holes in our plan. Bert didn't seem bothered.

"He'll be there, he's a mug. We need to figure out how we'll get into the Wilds without him seeing us."

"That'll be easy; we'll get there early and hide until it's time, there's loads of bushes around the side – we saw them from the viaduct, remember? Then we'll go back round, climb onto the bunker and watch him."

"Okay, we'll need to cover up, Theresa was right. Otherwise, we'll burn too. How early do you think?"

"One ish?"

"Sounds good," Bert was restless again, his feet tapping on the pavement. By the time the door of the house behind us opened and the lady shouted at us to get off her wall, we were ready to go anyway. The walking was considerably easier now the path was leading downhill.

"Shall we go for a swim?" Bert asked.

"Yeah, okay. I'll take Max back and get my stuff."

"I'll get mine and see you at the end of the road."

I knew that Bert was keeping me away from a potential meeting with Tubs, and I was grateful to him.

Inside the house, I had to step around the Hoover, which was standing in the middle of the hallway. I had left it there earlier to remind myself that it was on the list for today. I fleetingly considered rushing around and doing it now, but Bert would be waiting, so I left it for later.

The afternoon was uneventful, sitting on a beach packed with a million other people – none of whom tried to hurt us. Intermittently splashing in and out of the sea when we started to feel too hot in the baking sun. I mulled over the events of the morning. Now the wheels had been set in motion, there were nagging doubts in the back of my mind: what if it didn't work? What if Tubs found out it was us? What if…? All we were going to do was inconvenience Tubs for a short time, and if he did get to the bottom of it, then we would have poked the bear. I hoped his investigative skills were on par with his other limited cognitive abilities. Bert appeared to have no such reservations. He was just looking forward to the following afternoon.

"It'll be funny; we need to think about what we can do next. I want to really wind him up."

We walked back through the town, two suntanned boys with wet hair and towels rolled up and tucked under their arms, looking like they didn't have a care in the world. We were the epitome of what a summer holiday should look like.

I was still thinking about what other vengeance we could extract on Tubs when I got home. I was soon distracted when I was informed that if I didn't get the hoovering done pretty quickly, there would be 'all sorts of trouble'. I didn't know how many sorts of trouble there were, and I didn't want to find out today. Once the hoovering was done, I ate my tea and then made myself scarce before Mum could think of any other jobs that I could do. I was sitting on my bed reading The Hobbit. I was nearly halfway through and listening to the twins down the road playing 'it' around the parked cars. I heard the sound of their mum shouting to them to come in because it was their bedtime. As the groans and moans subsided, I remembered the tape Theresa had given me.

It had the same multi-coloured writing as before, this time, she had superimposed a picture of a banana over the track list, I had no idea why. It wasn't much like the Lou Reed tape and nothing at all like the David Bowie one. It was unlike anything I'd ever heard before;

loud, quiet, angry, sad – it did everything. Just when you thought you were getting the hang of it, it changed. I rewound Sunday Morning over and over, deciding it was my new favourite song and wondering why I had never heard it before.

***

After the incident with Tubs, Theresa had barely left the house. She had busied herself with things to do to distract her from what had happened on Ladybird Day. She was trying to force herself to forget that awful afternoon. This had only lasted a day before Janet sought her out. Theresa hadn't wanted to see her. She never wanted to see Tubs - or Alan - again and had no intention of accompanying Janet to any more of her lover's rendezvous. She had been thinking about how to break this to Janet without having to tell her about Shorts and Alan's revenge plan for Tubs. But now Janet was here on the doorstep - with streaks of mascara running down her cheeks and reddened eyes, what was she supposed to do?

Once she got Janet cleaned up, with a drink of squash in front of her, Janet had managed to choke back her tears (mostly) for long enough to tell Theresa what had happened. Unsurprisingly, Alan had broken up with her. Or, to be more specific, had told her he was going to break up with her. He had broken the news to her he would be moving away at the end of the holiday but wanted to stay together until then. He had told her brutally, but maybe truthfully, Theresa thought, that there would be no point after that.

Janet had stayed for over an hour, pouring her heart out, before finally going home to 'just be on her own for a while'. Theresa knew she shouldn't be relieved, but she was anyway.

It was a few days later before anybody else came to call. Claire was at home; she had been sitting in the garden with her for most of the morning before going to get ready for her afternoon shift. No sooner had she gone inside to get changed than Theresa heard the side gate open. She looked up to see Bert, Shorts and Max emerge from the side of the house.

She was, of course, happy to see them – especially Max, who seemed to remember her from the last time they met. After making an inordinate amount of fuss of him, she remembered her manners and got drinks for everyone, including Max. It occurred to her, while she was in the kitchen, that she was only wearing her bikini and that maybe she should cover up. But it was only Shorts and Bert, and they'd already been there for ages, so there didn't seem much point. It wasn't as though it was Tubs or anyone like that.

It was once the niceties and small talk were over that they finally revealed the reason for their visit. They told her about the bullying, which sounded awful, but there was something else, something neither of the boys seemed to want to tell her. She had no idea what else Tubs had done to upset them, and she didn't press them for any more than they had already told her. Considering what he had done the other day, nothing would surprise her. The fact that it was Tubs they were plotting against was good enough for her. She decided that she would go along with it, whatever, anything to help them get their revenge on him would be good. She would even get some revenge of her own by proxy.

Their plan was basic, to say the least. They appeared to have given little or no thought to any of the details. It was more of a vague outline of an idea. Despite this, the idea of Tubs sitting out in the blazing sun, being bitten by insects while he waited forlornly for a date that never came, appealed to her. He had scared and humiliated her the other day, and she wanted a little payback.

She added some refinements to their plan for them. Once that was done, she wrote a letter to Tubs on her best-writing paper. The letter was hard to write, after what he had done to her, it left a bad taste in her mouth to write something so intimate and suggestive to him. She knew it had to be convincing, or he would never turn up. She also knew it had to promise something that would be worth him turning up for. The anonymous letter purported to be from a secret admirer who thought Tubs was 'the best-looking boy in school'. They thought he was so big and strong and couldn't wait to feel his hands on her body. She thought Tubs would be an idiot if he believed it was real. But she was fairly certain he was an idiot, so it stood a chance.

After the obligatory sharing of tapes with Shorts, the boys and Max left, walking off into the hot afternoon like something out of an Enid Blyton book. Theresa returned to her place in the sun with more of a smile than she had had for days. Bert had been fairly quiet, but he usually was. Shorts had been his usual oddball self, even if she did notice him staring at her once or twice when he thought she wasn't looking.

When Claire got back from work that evening, she asked,

"Which one's your new friend, then?"

"Shorts, the one with short hair."

"Well, that makes it easy to remember, I liked his dog."

"Max, isn't he the cutest?"

"Well, for what it's worth, I approve of your new friend."

It was worth a lot, Theresa smiled to herself as her sister went upstairs to get changed out of her work clothes.

SEVENTEEN

I woke up early the next morning, a mixture of excitement and nervous anticipation made sure I could not stay in bed. It fuelled me through my morning walk with Max and my short list of chores – which I was specifically instructed to complete BEFORE I went out and did *'whatever it is you get up to all day'*. I had a little chuckle at that last bit, thinking that Mum would never guess in a million years what I was going to be 'getting up to' today.

Bert appeared in the middle of the morning. There was still plenty of time to kill, so we went for a brisk walk to the shops. We helped ourselves to some sweets, Bert asking about when the next Beano was going to be delivered while I slipped confectionary into my pockets. I wasn't sure, but I thought that the woman in the shop may have been watching me more closely than usual. It was probably just my imagination as I was feeling a bit on edge anyway, but maybe best to be a bit more careful for a day or two.

We wished away the minutes and the hours, wasting time in my room listening to tapes and reading comics until we finally couldn't help ourselves any more. Impatiently, we made our way towards the Wilds to find a place to conceal ourselves while we waited for Tubs to arrive - if he did. We wanted to make sure we were ready to witness his humiliation first-hand.

The walk was hot. The blazing afternoon sun notwithstanding, we were both wearing jeans and long-sleeved shirts as we had planned to protect ourselves from the sun, the bugs and the undergrowth. My shirt was not as long-sleeved as it had once been, it was an old favourite that I was rapidly growing out of. So far, it had escaped Mum's eagle eye and had been permitted a short reprieve from the rag bag. Bert's shirt was a brown patterned button-up shirt, the kind of fancy shirt I would never have been allowed to wear for playing out. He looked cool in it, almost as if he had dressed up for the occasion. We scrambled through the gap in the fence and followed the path to the bunker. We moved to the side that offered the most shade, then settled down on the dusty red ground with our backs to the rough concrete wall.

"What time do you think it is?" I asked Bert. We could see the town from where we were sitting, but not the church tower, with its huge clock that provided most of the kids in town with their only reliable form of timekeeping.

Bert pulled up a crisply ironed cuff and revealed a shiny Timex watch with a brown strap.

"One o'clock," he informed me.

Nice watch."

"Thanks, Dad got it for me for Christmas, I thought it might be useful today."

"Yeah, good thinking," I replied, secretly wondering if it might have been useful on other days as well, especially if it could have stopped me from getting in late for tea. My watch had come a cropper within a few weeks of my birthday, an incident with a tree and a rope swing will do that. I was dreading the inevitable day when Mum would suggest that I wear it, I would have to confess. For now, though, she seemed to have forgotten it so it could stay safely in the bottom of my underwear drawer.

There was still an hour to go before we would know if our plan had worked. A thought occurred to me,

"What if other kids turn up?"

"What other kids?"

"Any of the other kids that hang out here. That would mess it up"

"I suppose it would. There's nobody else here now, though, we'd hear them."

I listened carefully. Bert was right; I heard nothing but crickets, birds, distant traffic and the far-off sound of the train heading towards the station. It increased as it got closer, the sound of iron and steel grinding and squealing as the train came to a halt. The harsh, metallic noise carried across the Wilds, drowning out everything else.

It was at this point that our plan nearly came undone. Bert stood up,

"I need a pee," he announced as he faced the undergrowth and started to unzip his fly. He froze as the noise of the train subsided. We both heard the sound of a tuneless attempt to whistle the song Fernando from the other side of the hut. It was close, but not too close, and quickly started to recede as the whistler started to move inward toward the centre. We both knew it must be Tubs, even though we couldn't see him, who else would be coming into the Wilds on their own on a hot afternoon like this? And who else would make such a racket bashing through the undergrowth whistling an ABBA song?

The sound moved away, the train started to pull out of the station, and Bert let loose a stream of piss into the bushes. I waited for him to finish before asking what we should do next.

"Climb on the roof and see if it's him, of course," Bert replied as he walked around the hut to the door and climbed up its large metal hinges. I followed him, and we were quickly onto the roof, flat on our bellies, looking out towards the clearing where Tubs had been told he would be meeting his mystery date. My heart was beating fast now, and I still didn't truly believe that we would be invisible to him from the Grotty Grotto despite having seen the evidence with my own eyes.

Tubs emerged from the greenery at the side closest to us. He made straight for the nearest milk crate. It was clear he had made an effort for his date, a clean yellow shirt under his denim waistcoat accompanied by the widest pair of flares I had ever seen. He looked around the clearing, then, deciding everything was satisfactory for his liaison, pulled a packet of cigarettes from his pocket and lit one. After the first few puffs, he reached into his other pocket, pulling out a small bottle which he held up to the light, briefly examining the label, before taking a swig and pulling a face that gave the impression that he didn't like it that much.

"What's that?" I asked.

"Dunno, looks like whiskey or something," was the reply.

Undeterred, Tubs took another swig, longer this time, then replaced the bottle in his pocket and continued to smoke his cigarette.

Bert and I watched over the next hour as Tubs waited in the clearing, sniffing his armpits several times, scratching his balls and pacing around the edge of the clearing while looking along the various paths that led into it. We ducked low when he did this, worried that he might see us if he looked up in the right direction. But he never looked up in any direction; he was focused on the imminent arrival of his dream girl. We sniggered as we heard his butchered version of Fernando drifting through the afternoon haze, Bert had to stifle outloud laughter when the song was replaced with a tuneless rendition of Afternoon Delight. We were too young to know the word 'irony' but old enough to recognise it when we saw it.

By the time it reached two thirty, Tubs had taken his waistcoat off, smoked another cigarette and seemed to have drunk a significant amount from his bottle. His singing had increased in volume, and his tours of the clearing were not as steady as when he first arrived. He was talking out loud, and although what he was saying was largely inaudible, it was interspersed with an interesting range of shouted expletives.

I was hot by now. I thought Tubs would have realised that nobody was coming and given up, but he either didn't know what time it was or had more determination and resilience than I would have guessed. I looked over at Bert and saw the huge smile he'd started the afternoon with was still there. He was enjoying this.

"Shall we go soon?" I asked.

"Just a bit longer, I want to see his face when he realises."

So we waited, but we never did see his face when the truth of his situation hit him. He took several more swigs from his bottle and then started swaying alarmingly on his milk crate. We watched as he lowered himself carefully to the floor, put his waistcoat under his head and stretched out in the sun. I thought he might just be resting, but the unmistakable sound of snoring wafted over to us just before the arrival of the three o'clock train covered the sound. I looked at Bert, who said,

"Okay, I've seen enough now. He's going to get burnt to a crisp sleeping there. Serve him right, the bastard."

With that, he stood up and jumped off the roof, confident that the sound of the train would cover any noise he made. I remember being too scared to jump the last time we were here. I was still nervous now, but not so much that I didn't stand up and follow Bert to the ground. We left the Wilds together and walked around to the estuary. The tide was out, leaving a vast expanse of mud that we sat on the edge of, plucking stones from the ground and tossing them in looping arches away from us. The satisfying splat they made when they landed was more than enough reward for searching out continuously bigger stones and rocks.

We didn't talk about Tubs much. I think there was mutual consent that we had achieved the first part of our revenge. It had been oddly satisfying to watch him, but I had felt a hint of sadness, too, which I didn't understand. Maybe I do now. Now, I know what pathos is, but at the time, it puzzled me.

Our stone-throwing entertainment extended itself to throwing stones towards the groups of wading birds that were finding their tea at the shoreline. I didn't think of this as remotely cruel, given that we didn't even come close to hitting any of them. Every time a rock got vaguely near them, they just calmly up-sticks and moved a bit further down the water's edge, where they carried on with their mealtime.

By now, I was hot and hungry, and I suggested that we start to head towards home. Bert grudgingly agreed. He had wanted to go back and have another look at Tubs but saw my point when I said that it was possible that Tubs would be awake again by now. If he was, and he caught sight of us, he would definitely be in a very bad mood. We walked back to my house, where Bert declined my offer to come in. He carried on up the road, whistling a creditable version of Fernando as he went.

Inside, I went into the kitchen to get a drink of squash. This turned out to be bad timing as Mum was just about to start making apple crumble with our windfalls. I was roped in to help with peeling the apples, gouging out the disgusting black bits and the cores with their hidden promises of maggots. I thought I might get away after that. But we were having a family dinner tonight as Dad had called to say he would be on time for a change.

I peeled potatoes, laid the table, helped make the gravy and was ordered around the boiling kitchen while the radio churned out a dismal procession of songs that Mum sang along with. They were certainly not Lou Reed or David Bowie. Eventually, we heard the front door open, followed shortly by Dad coming into the kitchen demanding to know what the lovely smell was. Mum kissed him before we all sat at the table for our family dinner. It was an unhurried meal, with plenty of time to talk – although I was purposefully vague about the details of my day for obvious reasons. My apple crumble was as delicious as apple crumble always is, with condensed milk poured on top and an extra sprinkle of sugar. Everything was good. Dad announced that we would be getting another TV once the school holiday was over, and then he looked at me, all kind of serious. Apparently, they both felt bad because they hadn't been able to spend much time with me this summer. I didn't let on that I wasn't that bothered, I mean, it wasn't like I was a little kid that needed looking after, was it?

"I know it's been hectic this summer, I'm sorry," he shrugged, looked at Mum, then carried on, "How about I put the tent up in the garden next week? You and your friend Robert can have a campout before you have to go back to school."

I ignored the part where he got Bert's name wrong and the bit about going back to school. A campout! I ran around the table and hugged him.

"I'll take that as a yes, then shall I? Now, come on and help me tidy up here."

Just for once, I didn't mind clearing the table or helping with the dishes. We were getting a TV again, and I was having a campout, I couldn't wait to tell Bert tomorrow. I was already planning in my head what things we would need and what I would have to ask Mum to get for us – sausages for definite.

Me and Dad were just putting the last of the dishes away when we heard sirens in the distance. Dad pulled a face and said,

"Good grief, as if I don't hear them enough already."

He rolled his eyes at me comically before he stepped out into the back garden, looking over in the direction the sound was coming from. I followed him and looked up to see a thick column of black smoke rising into the air in the distance.

"Looks like it's at the train station," Dad said as we heard more sirens approaching. Then he put his hand on my shoulder, "I suppose I'll find out all about it when I get into work tomorrow. Come on, let's get these dishes finished up."

I took one last look at the plume of smoke that darkened the early evening sky before I followed him back inside. When we had finished, Dad went to sit with Mum in the lounge. I went upstairs. I had only just put my music on when Mum came in to shut my windows.

"I'm just keeping the smoke out," she told me, "I don't know what's going on, but it's all drifting this way."

Now she mentioned it, I realised that the burning smell had indeed started to invade my room, there had also been no let-up in the sounds of sirens. I looked out of the window towards the estuary and saw an eerie orange glow across the sky. Mum asked me what on earth I was listening to. I didn't tell her that the song was called Heroin, even at my young age, I realised that this would not be received well.

"It's a tape a friend made for me," I answered.

"Well, keep it down, won't you, goodnight."

I obligingly turned the volume all the way down from seven to five before settling down and reading my book.

EIGHTEEN

I couldn't wait to see Bert the next morning to tell him about the campout. My list of chores was small, because I'd helped with the tea last night I expect. I took Max for his daily constitutional in the park, he was as excited and happy as always to be there, sniffing and snuffling his way around the bushes and trees. I dropped by Bert's house on the way home. Max lay panting on the front path while I waited for Bert to answer the door. He eventually opened it just as I was about to give up. He was wearing a pair of blue and white striped pyjama bottoms, and his hair was unbrushed and wild. He offered a perfunctory greeting before turning and walking to the kitchen, leaving the door open for me to follow him. I shooed Max into the back garden while Bert poured some cornflakes and milk into a bowl and started eating. I helped myself to a drink of squash before telling him about the fire.

"I know," he answered, "down at the Wilds." He carried on eating his breakfast, which made me feel a bit hungry even though I'd already had mine.

"Shall we go down and have a look?"

"I went last night." This was simply stated; it did not answer my question, but it gave rise to another,

"When last night?"

"After I heard the fire engines, Mum was already in bed, so I snuck out to have a look."

I was shocked. The idea of going out without permission at night had never even occurred to me.

"What was it like?"

"A lot of fire engines with their lights flashing, firemen running around, that sort of thing. A lot of smoke, too." His answers were frustratingly succinct.

"I'm going to get dressed," he told me, but before he could get to the stairs, the phone rang. He detoured to the little table by the front door and answered it. I listened to his half of the conversation,

"Yeah…No, he's still in bed…I'll get him, he'll be pissed off, he's still in bed…OK, hang on."

He put the receiver next to the phone and went to the foot of the stairs,

"ALAN, IT'S FOR YOU."

He got no response so, muttering under his breath, he went up the stairs and banged his fist on his brother's door,

"Al, phone for you."

From where I was sitting in the kitchen, I could only hear the muffled response, inaudible but sounding like it could have been swearing. Bert answered,

"You tell him I'm getting dressed."

There was a tattoo of pounding feet and banging doors as Bert went into his room, and Alan got out of bed and crashed down the stairs to pick up the phone,

"If that's fucking Tubs, I'll kill him for ringing up this early."

He picked up the receiver,

"What? I was aslee..what?...What do you mean?...No, I haven't…Well, someone must."

For a moment, both ends of the conversation went quiet before Alan said,

"Okay, meet me at Jim's as soon as you can get there. I'm on my way."

He put the phone down and went back up the stairs with more bumps and crashes. Bert returned, clothed but still looking sleepy.

"What were they talking about?" he asked.

"Dunno, I could only hear half of it, something about going to Jim's."

He joined me at the kitchen table with a drink of his own as Alan came hurtling back down the stairs, he stood in the kitchen doorway,

"Have either of you seen Tubs?" he asked.

We both looked at him and shook our heads, which he barely acknowledged before rushing out of the front door, leaving it ajar behind himself.

"What was that about?" I asked Bert, "Do you think they know about what we did?"

"No, how could they?"

"I don't know, it's just a bit odd, that's all. What do you think's up?"

Bert didn't have a chance to answer before the phone rang again. He answered it and let the caller know that Alan wasn't there, then came back to the kitchen.

"We could go to the beach today," Bert suggested.

"Yeah, okay, can we walk past the Wilds, though?"

"Sure, why not? I don't think there'll be much left to see."

It turned out he was right about that, as we would find out later. I was collecting Max from the garden when Janet came in through the still-open front door. She looked flustered as if she had been running – or at least walking quickly. Like everybody else today, she seemed to have got dressed in a rush; her tee shirt was clearly inside out, and her hair was pulled back into a tiny ponytail.

"Is Alan upstairs?" she asked.

"No, he just went out," Bert told her.

"Where too?"

"Jim's house."

"Where's that?"

Bert told her, but she didn't leave, she stood in the kitchen doorway,

"Isn't it terrible?" she asked us.

I looked at Bert blankly before asking what it was that was terrible.

"About Tubs, they think he was in the Wilds last night when it burnt down."

My blood ran cold, I couldn't answer Janet's question – and I had no idea what I would say if I did. Bert stepped in,

"That is awful, are they sure?"

"Not yet, but nobody's seen him since yesterday. I hope he's okay."

She looked as if she was about to cry, and then she turned and left without saying anything else, leaving me staring at Bert across the table. There was a silence which hung between us for a fraction too long before I asked,

"Is it our fault?"

Bert did not make eye contact with me,

"They don't even know if it's him yet, he may have just got lost somewhere."

I couldn't imagine where Tubs would get lost in our small town, but I didn't argue about it.

"What if they find out about the note and everything?"

Now Bert did look at me,

"It'll be all burnt up now if Tubs was still in the Wilds. The only way anyone would know about it is if we tell them. We didn't do anything wrong; it was just a joke. Don't say anything – to anyone."

The last part was given as an order, not a suggestion. It did nothing to quell my fear that we had done a dreadful thing, although the last time I saw Tubs, he had been sleeping peacefully, so Bert was probably right.

We did walk past the Wilds on our way to the beach, and there was nothing much to see apart from a lot of people in various uniforms, a lot of other people who had 'just happened' to walk that way and the top of a white tent just visible above the tips of the blackened and charred remains of the vegetation. The bunker was sooty and blackened, standing alone and proud, the tired paint on the door now blistered and peeling. The area surrounding it was providing a small space for firemen to stop and compare notes.

On the beach, we found that we had little to say, both locked in with our thoughts and worries. Bert did not seem to want to talk about what had happened or speculate on the events of the night. I guessed he was worried about his brother's friend, which I thought was weird, considering how mean Tubs had been to us. By early afternoon, we had both had enough and decided to call it a day, walking back a different way from the route we had taken on the way there, by mutual unspoken agreement, avoiding passing the Wilds again.

By the time I got home, I was tired. I slumped on my bed with some music on. The Hobbit rested in my lap, open but unread. I couldn't concentrate on the words or the music, though. I had convinced myself that it was true, that Tubs had been in the Wilds last night. I was busy worrying that we may have contributed to what happened to him in some way. Bert was right, though, how could we have been? It was three in the afternoon when we were there, and the fire engines didn't start arriving until after tea.

I had just about made peace with myself and started reading again when the doorbell rang. I assumed it was Bert, I went to the top of the stairs and shouted to him to come in. The door opened tentatively, and, to my surprise, Theresa stepped into my hallway, looking up the staircase at me with red eyes.

I knew she was upset, but I still couldn't stop myself from thinking how nice she looked in a sun dress with blue and white diagonal stripes and her hair tied into pigtails. I wasn't sure what to do; no girls had ever called for me before, and I had little to no experience of dealing with people who were upset.

"How did you know where I live?" I asked.

"The phone book Shorts, I looked it up."

Now I felt stupid, I should and could have thought of that. I struggled to think of what to say next, Theresa helped me out,

"Can I come in?"

"Oh yeah, sure. Come on up."

I looked back into my room and immediately wished I had suggested sitting downstairs instead. I was pushing the worst of the debris to one side with my foot when Theresa came in. She sat on the end of my bed and looked at me,

"You know what happened, don't you?"

"What, about Tubs?"

"Yes."

"Have they found him?"

"They've found a body in the Wilds. They don't know if it is him yet, but it is, isn't it?"

She started to cry again. Again, I didn't know what to do, so I sat on the other end of the bed. I had been telling myself that it was some kind of mix-up, that Tubs was going to turn up and start tormenting me again the next time I left the house. I didn't ask how she knew about them finding the body, and I didn't doubt it either, my feelings from earlier flooded back.

"Is it our fault?" Theresa asked.

"I don't see how it can be. He was asleep in the Grotty Grotto when we left. That was hours before the fire; he must have gone back there for something later."

"But it was us that made him go there in the first place."

"Yeah, but not in the evening. We were only playing a joke."

Theresa looked at me, and tears were rolling down her cheeks,

"I feel like it was my fault," she said, "he wouldn't have gone there if it wasn't for us."

I remembered what Bert had said about not telling anyone, and I knew that was the best thing to do. Even so, I felt tears welling in my own eyes.

"But we didn't mean for anything bad to happen, only you, me and Bert know about it. If we don't tell anybody, it'll be fine."

Theresa looked doubtful, but when she saw that I was upset too, she moved up the bed and put her arm over my shoulders. For the first time since the morning, I felt a little bit less shitty. I knew what we had done was wrong, but I still couldn't see how it would be our fault.

"Okay, shorts," said Theresa, rubbing her eyes with the back of her hand, "our secret, the three of us. But if anybody asks me, I think I'll have to own up; I'm not good at lying. Are you okay?"

Her arm was still around me, her body leaning against mine, and it felt warm and soft and good. I didn't want to tell her I was okay because I didn't want her to move away.

"I guess so; I don't know, really."

She took her arm off my shoulders anyway and nodded towards the tape player where Nico was singing, 'You're put down in her book, You're number thirty-seven have a look.'

"How are you liking it?"

"I love it, did they do any other albums?"

"Yes, I'll tape them for you. My sister can get most things from work."

I felt a pang of jealousy. It must be good to have a sister who had access to such a cool music library.

"That'd be good."

"I made a tape for you today," she said, producing it from her pocket. "In case anybody asked why I was coming here."

I liked that level of planning. I thought again about how poor mine and Bert's scheming had been. This made me sad again, thinking about how badly our plan had turned out. I turned away from Theresa, not wanting her to see me crying again, I changed the tape in the player for the one she had just given me.

I read the box; one side was another David Bowie album, Hunky Dory, I hoped it was as good as the last one. The other side was by someone called Patti Smith, who I'd never heard of. I was already looking forward to listening to it. Downstairs, I heard the door open and Mum coming in,

"I'd better get going, Shorts, I'll see you soon, okay?"

"Yeah, I'll let you out."

It was after I had said goodbye to Theresa that I found out that we had a house rule about not having girls in the bedroom, who knew? I went back up and listened to the tape. Bowie was great, and Horses was weird but kind of interesting, too. I would need to listen to it again before I made my mind up whether I liked it or not. I did not hear from Bert again for several days.

***

Theresa stood on the pavement for a moment, looking at Shorts' house. She didn't know if this was the right thing to do, but she had to do something. Tonight was going to be awful; as if the constant heat and humidity weren't already enough to keep her awake all night, she would now have added thoughts about Tubs to stop her from sleeping again tonight. Or, more specifically, Tubs' death and whether she was partly to blame. She had decided, during the day, that she probably was and knew she had to talk to someone about it. Even though she could usually talk to Claire about anything, she didn't think she could tell her this. So Shorts was the someone, if she was to blame, then so was he. Although, what she wanted most was for it to be neither of them.

She could have gone to see Bert, of course, but the strong likelihood of bumping into Alan stopped her from doing that. She didn't know if she could look Alan in the eye without her guilt being completely obvious to him. She knew she couldn't talk to Janet about it either. Besides, Shorts was easier to talk to than Bert or Janet.

As soon as he opened the door, she could see that he was as worried as she was, which did little to assuage her fears. She followed him upstairs, and they talked, sitting on the bed in his cluttered room. The tape player and tapes took pride of place, and she was amused to see that he had tried to copy the style of the writing on the cassette boxes she had lent him. She wondered if maybe she should offer to do them for him in future.

Aside from this, the room was crowded with comics, toys, model planes and the sort of random objects that boys appeared to accumulate around themselves. A slightly tatty bear peered out forlornly from under the pillow, the walls were decorated with pictures of Dr Who and his companion, Sarah Jane, carefully cut from magazines. They were interspersed with a selection of surprisingly good, hand-drawn pictures of the Dr's various adversaries. Daleks, Cybermen, and Zygons stared down at her, bringing back memories of Saturday evenings peering out from behind cushions.

When she told him about Tubs, it was clear that he had been trying to convince himself that everything would be okay, that Tubs would turn up swearing, all fists and sneers. When she plucked up the courage to ask if it was their fault, he was adamant that it was not, that Tubs must have returned to the Grotto in the evening.

"What about the note?" she had asked.

Shorts told her that they had seen Tubs take the letter from his pocket when him and Bert had been spying on him as they giggled in the afternoon. The time when everything was still nothing more than a cruel practical joke. He had put the pink sheet of paper down on one of the milk crates, and it would have certainly been cremated in the blaze if he had left it there. There was nothing to link them with Tubs' presence in the Grotto.

She didn't know if he was trying to convince her or himself. Whichever it was, he was upset. They comforted each other as best they could because sometimes you just need to hold on tightly to someone. The tears had come for both of them, hot and cathartic, binding them together in their conspiracy of silence.

She walked home the long way, avoiding the top gate where the incident with Tubs had taken place. Probably, she was not even aware that she had done this. Eventually, she would start using that route again – but not yet, the town still had to get used to Tubs' absence. In time it would, in a few years, the Wilds would be bulldozed to make space for a new road to run alongside the railway track. Nobody would notice or care that Tubs final resting place had been tarmacked over, and he would be forgotten, just like the Freeman kid who had drowned the previous year.

NINETEEN

It felt as if a dark cloud hung over the town despite the blue sky and bright sunshine. The news of Tubs' death spread as fast as the fire that had engulfed him through the bush telegraph of gossip and rumours that exist in small communities up and down the country - she said, he said, did you hear? Word got around, and it was the only thing that people were talking about in the hours and days following the fire.

I was terrified that there would be a knock on the door at any moment. Positive I would be confronted by a stern-faced police officer who would ask if I had sent Tubs to his death. I knew that when that happened to me, I would crumble and confess everything, letting my guilt and shame flood out. But for now, it was buried deep inside, my shared secret eating away beneath the surface like a malevolent parasite. I managed to convince myself that this was what had happened to Bert, who I hadn't seen since the trip to the beach the morning after the fire. I was certain that he had been driven away in the back of a police car and was being interrogated in a bare room lit with a single light bulb.

When I did eventually venture out to find Bert, his house was shut up tight; nobody answered the door, and there were no signs of life inside when I peered through the window. I disconsolately walked onwards towards what remained of the Wilds. As I approached, the smell of charred and burnt vegetation still hung in the air. The pavement was so blasted by the heat that even the weeds had shrivelled to nothing but dry wisps of grass and yellowed leaves. As soon as the railings came into sight, with their paint now hanging off in shreds and tatters, I panicked and turned back for home.

There was a part of me that wanted to talk to Theresa again, while another part of me reasoned that we had already said what we needed to say. I kept thinking about her after her surprise visit, wondering how she felt about me and how I felt about her. I had decided that she was possibly the most beautiful girl I knew, but I was unsure about how I should let her know this. This was all uncharted territory for me.

Then, an idea occurred to me: the kind of inspiration that makes you feel proud of yourself even if nobody else witnesses it. Music was mine and Theresa's 'thing'. If I got her a tape, I'd have a reason to visit her – and we'd have something to talk about apart from Tubs dying in the fire. This changed quickly from an idea to an actual plan, at the very least, it would fill the empty day. I changed direction and started to walk towards the shops, no longer trudging but now striding purposefully.

Arriving at my destination, I did my very best nonchalant browse, looking at various random items and objects as I sauntered towards the rear of the shop, where the music lived. Once I was in front of the rack of tapes, I realised, belatedly, that I had no idea what Theresa would want. The bewildering array of titles on offer was spread out before me – Ziggy Stardust in front of me, The Velvet Underground away to my right. At least now, the reason for the carefully drawn banana on my cassette cover made sense.

I looked through the multitude of rectangular cases, hoping to glean some insight into their contents from the covers and the track listings. The only thing I was reasonably sure of was that Showaddywaddy was probably not what I was looking for. I was immersed in reading the track listing on Jailbreak by Thin Lizzy, so I didn't notice someone coming up behind me until they spoke,

"You're not thinking of nicking that, are you?"

My heart leapt into my mouth as I rushed to put the tape back as hastily as I could. I turned around, ready to deny that I would do any such thing. As I turned, I saw the smiling face of Not Theresa, the bigger, older version of her. She smiled broadly as I answered,

"No, I wasn't going to nick it, I was just looking."

"Good," she answered, "it's crap. You're Theresa's little friend, aren't you?"

I agreed that I was, she must have remembered me from when she had opened the door to me and Bert when we visited Theresa to formulate our ill-fated plan.

"Well, you shouldn't buy them anyway. I get a discount, and Theresa will make you a copy of anything good that comes out - if you ask her nicely." Again, a grin, followed by her reaching past me and plucking Station To Station from the display,

"Has she given you this yet?"

I said that she hadn't, only Ziggy Stardust and Hunky Dory, Theresa's sister rolled her eyes and made a face,

"Well, that's a good start, tell her you want this next. It's so much better than some of the tired old rubbish that's out now." She waved her hand across the tapes in front of us, then carried on,

"You should go and see her; she's been down since the fire last week. I think she's fallen out with Janet, too; you might be able to cheer her up."

"Okay," I answered, "I might do that."

So, the tape idea had been blown out of the water, but now I had another valid reason to visit Theresa, namely that her sister had told me to. I thought about the long, hot walk up the steep hill and decided that I would put it off until tomorrow. I'd take Max with me; he would like the walk, and Theresa would be pleased to see him if not me.

Decision made, I returned home, through the heat of the afternoon, to the coolish shade of my room. I was copying a picture of a tank onto my roll of paper when the phone rang. I jumped up to answer it, but Dad – who I hadn't realised was in – came out of the sitting room and picked it up as I got to the top of the stairs. Naturally, I stopped and listened on the off chance that it might be for me. It wasn't, it was Dad's work friend, Bill. The conversation was brief, and I could only hear one side of it, but it was evidently about the fire at the Wilds and about Tubs. I waited for them to finish their conversation, then as Dad put the phone down, I came down the stairs and asked,

"Did they find out who did it?"

"What?"

"Whose fault it was that Tubs died?"

He looked confused for a moment, then made the connection,

"You mean Clive, the boy who died in the fire?"

I hadn't realised that his real name was Clive, but I agreed that we were talking about the same person.

"Well, it was nobody's fault," he had guided me to the kitchen, where we sat at the table, and he explained to me that Tubs had been drinking and smoking. The investigation team were pretty sure that he dropped a cigarette in the bushes while he was in the clearing, he fell asleep after drinking some whiskey, and probably never even knew what happened. He then reminded me of the dangers of smoking, drinking, playing in places that I wasn't supposed to and fires in general.

"Now," he said, "I've got a job for you to help me with."

My heart sank, a moment ago, my world had improved by about a thousand per cent, now I had been cornered by Dad to help with more chores. Nevertheless, I asked what he wanted me to do, hoping it wasn't anything to do with cleaning the car – probably not because of the water shortage.

"You can help me lift the tent down from the loft, then put it up in the garden."

I didn't have time to say anything before he went on to explain,

"I've got a few days off. I thought you could have your campout in the garden this week."

This would be a great end to the summer. I asked if Bert could still come too, and Dad said the whole bloody street could come if I wanted, but I'd have to put the tent up first. Together, we collected the bundle of poles, blue canvas and strings from the attic and assembled a slightly musty-smelling, faded-at-the-top tent in the middle of the back lawn. Dad did most of it, me and Max tried to assist as best we could, although Max seemed even more excited than me and mostly just barked, got in the way and tangled himself in guy ropes. Once it was complete, Dad stood next to me and said,

"We'll let it air a bit, you can sleep out tomorrow, okay?"

It was more than okay. It was fantastic. I hugged him and then went in to make two glasses of squash for us, then one for Mum, as she had just arrived home, too. Then I tore another page from my school book, which I used to write a note inviting Bert to join me. After being admonished for my poor handwriting and atrocious spelling, I went and posted it through his letter box. The house was still empty. I hoped he would be back from wherever he had got to in time for tomorrow night.

TWENTY

I was up early the next morning. I started the day with a trip to town to collect the list of things I would need for the campout. Mum had given me some money to get bread rolls and sausages, plus some extra for sweets and new batteries for my torch. There were also some opportunistic demands from Mum for other items that had nothing to do with my campout, but I didn't mind getting them today. On my way home with the shopping, I passed Bert's house, but it still looked empty, and nobody answered my knocking. I returned home, unpacked the shopping and clipped Max's lead onto his collar.

The walk up to Theresa's house was every bit as steep, hot and tiring as it had been the last time I went. I hoped Theresa would be in and that the trip would not all be for nothing. I was relieved as I approached the house, I could hear music coming from inside, at least someone was at home to answer the doorbell.

Theresa looked surprised when she saw me, then delighted as she bent down to make the usual fuss over Max before inviting us in. Max's tail was at full speed, and he went straight through to the garden to sniff around the borders and edges while Theresa got us both a cold drink. She had a vest top with two large flowers embroidered on the front and a pair of white flared trousers that rested in folds on her bare feet.

"Your sister said I should come and see you," I explained. Theresa looked at me with raised eyebrows, and I continued, "I saw her in

Smiths yesterday, she said you'd been sad, and I should come and cheer you up."

"Did she? Well, she wasn't wrong. So, can you cheer me up?"

"I can, actually," I told her. I then repeated what Dad had told me about the fire and Tubs, about it being Tubs' fault because he was smoking and drinking. Theresa still looked unsure,

"Yeah, but he wouldn't have been there if it wasn't for us."

"No, but we didn't make him do the other things, did we?"

"No, but…" she paused, then smiled, "No, you're right, that was him, wasn't it?"

I was glad to see that I had managed to achieve my goal of putting her mind at rest about our role, or lack of it, in Tubs' death. I smiled back and realised that I was starting to feel better about it too, now that I had shared my information. I couldn't wait to tell Bert when I saw him next, hopefully tonight.

"Also, I continued, "your sister said you should tape Station to Station for me. She said it was the best thing to come out this year."

"It's about the only good thing that has come out this year, haven't you got it?"

"No."

"Come on upstairs, we'll tape it now."

"Am I allowed in your room?" I asked, remembering the recently discovered rule in my own home. Theresa gave me an odd look and answered,

"Of course, why wouldn't you be?"

I wasn't sure, but I was happy to go upstairs with her anyway.

Girls' bedrooms are so different. I mean, I knew girls were different, obviously. But it hadn't occurred to me that they would live in such a different space from us boys. Mine and Bert's rooms still held the detritus of our childhoods, toys and annuals, models and comics, all spaced and placed conveniently around the room so they could be easily accessed. Our minimal wardrobes were tucked into corners, and the beds were usually unmade and functional.

But here, in Theresa's bedroom, was a revelation. It was mostly pink, with flowers on the wallpaper and a small desk with various tubes and pots sitting in front of a mirror, sharing the space with colouring pens and pencils and a pad of paper. The bedspread was a light purple colour with a ruffled frill and matching pillowcase, and there were clothes draped and folded, spilling out of the drawers and wardrobe to spread around the room. On the floor, next to the wardrobe, was a music centre, a record player with a built-in tape recorder and a radio. This was surrounded by piles of tapes and albums, one of which I could clearly see was by Showaddywaddy. I decided not to mention that as Theresa found a blank tape and started to record the David Bowie album that her sister had said I should have a copy of.

"I'm having a campout tonight," I told her. She gave me an odd look.

"What in a tent?"

"Yes, in the garden."

"Why?"

"It'll be fun. I wanted Bert to come, but he's not around."

"He'll be back later," Theresa informed me.

"How do you know?"

"Janet told me. Their mum has taken Alan and Bert to see their new house."

This was news to me,

"What new house?"

"You know, the house in…" she looked at me and stopped speaking for a moment. Her expression changed as she started again,

"Didn't Bert tell you? They're moving to Plymouth. Their mum has a new job. Janet's heartbroken, of course, even though they've only been going out for a few weeks. I'm trying to avoid her because she keeps crying."

I didn't know what to say, why hadn't Bert told me this? Was it even true? What was I supposed to do without Bert? I kind of knew how Janet felt. Theresa saw how upset I must have looked.

"Don't you start crying too, I'm sorry, did you really not know?"

I shook my head. For the second time that week, Theresa put her arm around my shoulders,

"Hey, it's okay, I'm pretty sure you'll still be able to write to each other or phone."

That wasn't the issue, who was I going to go out and mess around with now? Where would I hang out when Mum was getting on my nerves - or arguing with Dad?

"You can always call round here if you need someone to listen to records with," she offered. "Come on, let's go and see what Max is up to while that finishes recording."

We went downstairs and had a drink and some biscuits, including Max, who wolfed his down even faster than me. I decided that there may be an upside to Bert leaving, spending time with Theresa and her biscuits for a start. I still felt pretty betrayed, though. When the tape was finished, and Theresa had made a suitably ornate cover for it, I went back down the hill. Theresa's parting words were,

"Pop round any time, Shorts."

This was an invitation that I decided I would take her up on despite the steepness of the hill, which didn't seem too bad on the way home.

***

It had been a relief when she opened the door to see Shorts standing there. She nearly hadn't answered it, fearful that it would be Janet again. She had spent two tiresome hours with her friend the day before, mostly listening to her crying. Her patience had started to wear thin after the first thirty minutes, meaning that the rest of the time, she had been in purgatory. She had been trying to discretely look at the clock and hoping that something would happen that would require her urgent presence elsewhere. Sadly, there was no such divine intervention.

Janet had talked about how dreadful it was about Tubs, what an awful way to die. This did nothing to make Theresa feel any better about what had happened. She had seen Tubs' sisters being interviewed on the news, their pallid faces streaked with mascara, lips trembling and holding on to one another as if they had lost the most precious thing in their lives. In reality, everybody knew what a hard time they gave Tubs when he was alive, not that that excused his behaviour or made his death more bearable.

But mostly, Janet had been bemoaning the fact that Alan was moving away, how unfair it was, and how much she was going to miss him. When she had finally run out of things to say about the tragedy of losing the love of her life, she started to cheer up a bit. There was another boy, Charles, that she fancied. She was hoping he would be in some of the same classes as her next year so she could get to know him better. Theresa knew what this meant, an all-out assault like the one Janet had made on Alan, where all dignity and self-respect were abandoned in pursuit of her target. She agreed that Charles was gorgeous and that Janet should ask him out when school restarted. What she actually wanted was for Janet to shut up and go away. She didn't, not straight away. Theresa was forced to listen to some lurid fantasies about what Charles might or might not get up to once Janet got him on his own in the snogging shelter in the park.

Theresa knew that she was going to spend less time with Janet next year, maybe continue to cultivate the new group of friends she had started to mix with last year. She did not doubt that Janet would revert to her other friends, Sue and Michelle, the moment school started back, it was a relief to know that she wasn't going to have to listen to her for too much longer.

She had been thinking of Shorts when the doorbell rang, wondering what part he might play in her new friendship group. When he had told her that Claire had sent him, she thought she couldn't love her sister any more than she already did, although she still had her eye on the bigger bedroom when it became available in the coming weeks.

Shorts had been almost ecstatic when he passed on the information about Tubs. If the fire brigade thought that was what had happened, they were probably right. She felt a weight lifting from her as this new information began to sink in, the quiet joy that comes with absolution. It seemed like a good way to end the holiday, not only was Tubs, with his grubby, groping hands and bad breath, gone, but it was not her fault either – even though she had wished him dead on the day he had attacked her. It was that wish that had made her feel the most guilty as if she had somehow made it happen through her bad thoughts.

Seeing Shorts, seeing Max, spending some time rifling through her music collection and sharing her favourite songs and artists had been cathartic. Shorts seemed to be soaking up every musical offering she gave him. It was like shaping a lump of clay or starting on a blank page. She was delighted to have someone who shared her tastes, unlike most of the people she knew who were still listening to disco shit or heavy metal.

The joy of Shorts' visit took a sharp downward turn when she told him that Bert and Alan were moving away. She had assumed, wrongly, that he already knew. Being the harbinger of such upsetting news had been hard, as Shorts was obviously very dismayed when she broke the news to him. She understood the two of them had been inseparable last year; you never saw one without the other. By the time Shorts and Max left, he had cheered up a bit; she hoped it wasn't going to spoil his planned campout with Bert.

TWENTY-ONE

Bert was sitting on the front wall waiting for me when I got back. I saw him as I walked down the road, I was busy planning in my head what I was going to say to him. As I arrived, he was smiling from ear to ear, and he held up a backpack and a tightly rolled sleeping bag,

"Campout, great idea, Shorts. I'm ready."

I wasn't going to be deterred or distracted from what I had decided to say,

"Why didn't you tell me you were moving house?" I blurted.

His expression shifted immediately from joy to a grimace.

"Because I hoped I could get Mum to change her mind, but I couldn't. She really wants her new job, and she'll be on more money. Also, she wants Alan to get a new start and buckle down to his school work – fat chance."

"When are you moving?"

"Next week," his expression perked up again, "so let's make the most of our campout."

I knew he was right; we should enjoy ourselves while we could, but it didn't stop me from feeling the saddest I could ever remember being. Even when Grandad died a couple of years ago, it wasn't like this. I forced myself to return his stupid grin and said,

"Come on, come and see the tent. We've got hot dogs, and Mum's going to make hot chocolate for us later."

We went through the house and into the back garden, where Bert gave his seal of approval to the tent by throwing his backpack and sleeping bag inside before sitting down in the doorway, where I joined him.

"Sorry I didn't tell you about moving," he said, "I was kind of hoping we wouldn't have to go."

Even though I was sad, I managed to respond with,

"What's the new house like?"

Bert became enthused as he began to describe his prospective home, with its spooky cellar, attic and massive garden,

"It's got a huge tree that I reckon I could climb, but I didn't get a chance to try it out yet."

"How far away is it?" I had little idea of distances or travel times, "maybe I could come for a visit?"

"Yeah, that would be great, it's quite a long way, though, it's nearly in Cornwall. It took us ages to get there. I'll probably have to come back and visit my old man sometimes, though, we could meet up then."

I agreed that this was probably the best idea, although the way Bert said 'have to' made me think it might not be that frequent.

We messed around for the rest of the afternoon. I cadged some more money off of Dad while he was in a good mood, and we went and got some more batteries, for the tape player this time. We set it up in the tent, where Dad had spread out all the spare blankets from the airing cupboard. He said it would make the rock-hard ground more comfortable, but I was dubious about his claim. Anyway, it wasn't as if anybody was using the blankets right now, so it was worth a try. We spread ourselves out on top of our sleeping bags and arranged our bags, torches, biscuits and sweets around us. I left my bear, Mr Panda, stuffed down the side of my bed upstairs, deciding it might not be cool in front of Bert. I would reinstate him later when I moved back inside.

Dad came out and started shifting a bag of logs around the garden, and it took me a moment to realise what he was doing. When I did, me and Bert rushed to help.

"Are we going to have a campfire?"

"You can't have a campout without one," Dad told us solemnly, "can you?"

Of course, with him being a fireman, it had to be done properly. He directed me and Bert to lay two paving slabs beside each other and make a small ring of bricks to keep the fire contained. Even before we had thought about lighting a fire, I was sent to collect a bucket of water to set next to it – just in case. Everything was a safe distance from both the house and the tent, which meant that it was practically at the bottom of the garden. Still, it was better than no campfire at all.

As the day wore on and evening approached, Mum cooked up the sausages in the kitchen. Me and Bert sat on the sparse grass, eating one hot dog after another, washing them down with a bottle of cherryade that we took turns to swig from. It was a truly memorable feast for what might be our last meal together for some time.

We sat and talked about the nothing and nonsense that twelve-year-old boys find to talk about, along with lashings of Monty Python quotes that had us laughing out loud despite the number of times we had heard them – or maybe because of that. We had whole sketches memorised and regurgitated them enthusiastically, with the swear words spoken quietly – in case Mum or Dad happened to be nearby. All the while, there was an unspoken undercurrent of sadness, a fragile thing that would surely ruin the evening if either of us thought too hard about Bert's impending move. We had neither the experience nor the tools to explore this, so we buried it.

Eventually, the sun started to dip, the shadows grew longer, and the temperature started to cool. Not a lot, but then it had been another sun-blasted day of record-breaking temperatures, according to the radio that we could hear from the kitchen window. It made the stuffy confines of the tent marginally more comfortable. Insects flitted, looking for one last stopping place for the evening, and birds called noisily from their sequestered roosting places as they wound down for the day.

Dad came and piled some twigs on top of a piece of newspaper in the centre of the brick circle. He lit the paper, then started to place larger pieces of wood on top as the fire began to take hold. Everything was tinder dry, and the flames were soon flicking upwards, spitting sparks towards the darkening sky and creating a small circle of light and heat where we sat and watched the shapes dancing while we fed sticks into the glowing embers. Dad supervised us from the shed, where he was studiously pretending to clean the lawn mower, even though he hadn't had to use it for weeks.

As the fire started to settle down, Mum came out with a tray of mugs, each one with a tiny lick of steam rising from it. Dad carried two deck chairs out of the shed for him and Mum, and we all sat together around the fire. The flames cast a yellow glow on our faces, leaving the gardens and houses behind us in a pool of shadow. There was some polite conversation about what good boys we had been this summer and whether were we looking forward to going back to school. Which was a stupid question, really, especially as Bert told them he would be going to a new school when he moved house. They asked some questions about that, questions that I should have asked if only I'd thought to, while our hot chocolate cooled down enough for us to take tentative sips without scalding our lips.

Eventually, we finished our drinks, Mum and Dad went inside, leaving us a list of instructions; 'don't forget to damp down the fire', 'remember to come in and brush your teeth later', 'don't make too much noise' and 'don't stay up too long'.

We agreed to all the terms and conditions, went inside to put our pyjamas on, and then slid into our sleeping bags with our heads sticking out through the open flap of the tent. As the sky continued to fade to a star-speckled purple ceiling, with a sliver of moon dangling over the roofs of the nearby houses, I decided that life probably couldn't be any better than this.

Bert ruined the moment when he asked who I might hang out with next term when I went back to school. I didn't want to think about Bert leaving or about going back to school. I didn't dislike the other boys at school, I just didn't like any of them enough to make a commitment. Besides, what if they didn't want to hang out with me? It felt wrong to discuss who would be Bert's replacement while he was still here, so I tried to change the subject.

"I saw Theresa this morning."

"Aha! So that's who you're going to be hanging out with then," he replied, then started making kissing noises on the back of his hand while he waggled his eyebrows up and down. I laughed because Bert always knew how to make me laugh, but I was also a bit embarrassed, so I told him to shut up. I immediately regretted it, as Bert seemed to amplify the noises he was making, he turned his back to me, wrapped his arms around himself and started running his hands up and down his back. I tried to change the subject again,

"I told her it wasn't our fault."

This finally got Bert's attention, he stopped what he was doing and rolled back to face me,

"What?"

I told him, repeating what Dad had said about Tubs, about the fire and the drinking and cigarettes. Bert stayed quiet, he lay on his front and looked up at the stars. The silence wasn't uncomfortable, despite the closeness of the darkened neighbouring houses, it felt as if I was floating in a sea of ink.

"You okay?" I asked.

He still didn't say anything, so I turned my head to look at him,

"What's up?"

He returned my gaze. His face was barely lit by the torch we had hung from the tent pole over the doorway. The shadows seemed to be running down his face like black tears.

"We hated him, though, right?"

"Yeah, I hated his guts."

"So it doesn't matter that he's dead then, does it?"

I didn't know what to say. It was true that I wasn't sad that he'd died – especially now that nobody was going to blame me. But I didn't know if I had wanted him dead, and a part of me suspected that it might matter to someone despite the bad things he had done.

"I suppose not," I answered.

Bert didn't say anything else for a bit. He returned to gazing at the sky as I continued to wonder if it really didn't matter. When he did speak again, it was in a quiet, barely audible whisper,

"But what if it wasn't an accident?"

"It was though, my Dad said that they are sure. He dropped his cigarette when he was drunk and didn't notice."

"Yeah," a distant car interrupted the silent pause, "but what if that wasn't what happened?"

"I don't get it, Dad said…"

"I know, but what if your dad and all the others were wrong?"

The idea of Dad being wrong about something had never really occurred to me before, about anything. Bert continued,

"What if someone saw Tubs sleeping there, in the clearing in the middle of the Wilds, and decided it would be funny to give him a scare?"

Bert had his eyes closed; his voice had become slower and quieter, and it was now hard to hear without straining.

"What if they set the bushes on fire so they could watch him run away screaming? But he didn't wake up, he just lay there. Then the bushes all went up in flames like the paraffin did that time by the garages, and there was nothing he could do to stop it once it had started."

He had rolled back onto his side, facing away from me, and his voice had started to quaver as he finished speaking.

"But we went home, we were gone ages before the fire," I said.

"You went home, Shorts," he replied, and I realised he was right, I had just assumed that Bert went home too, after he left me.

"But that wasn't what happened. It was an accident. Tubs did it himself."

"Okay," Bert murmured, "that's good."

We lay in silence. At some point, I must have fallen asleep. I awoke to see the torch glowing a feeble yellow light as it sucked the last remnants of life from its drained batteries. The sky had begun to lighten at its edges, light enough for me to see the dew that had formed on the struggling blades of grass, giving them a taste of the moisture that they had been so desperate for this long hot summer.

I looked at the shadowy lump that was Bert, breathing gently inside his sleeping bag, and thought about what he had said. What if someone had done that? What if someone had deliberately started the fire that killed Tubs? Would I still be off the hook? Or would I be even more to blame than I had been before? And what if that someone was Bert? It wasn't possible. I knew Bert, and he wouldn't do a thing like that – would he?

I thought there was little chance of sleeping again now, I lay and watched the sky gradually and imperceptibly brighten as the sun crept upwards, ready to banish the shadows and chase away the tortured thoughts of the dead of night. The birds began to greet the new day, slowly at first, then increasing in volume as the sun lit the world with its promise of another scorching day. The gulls were less coy, noisily claiming the morning as their own, like they always did.

Despite this, I must have dozed off again as the next thing I was aware of was Mum, standing in the front of the tent in bright sunshine carrying two plates, each with a bacon sandwich made from thick chunks of bread with ketchup dripping down their sides. Bert yawned himself awake, having been oblivious to my sleepless night, and started to tuck into his sandwich hungrily. Once finished, we padded across the wet grass, leaving a trail of footprints across the floor as we went inside to dress and use the bathroom.

"What do you want to do today?" I asked, quietly hoping that Bert would want to go home.

"Sorry, Shorts, I promised Mum I would help start packing our stuff up," he answered, making me feel guilty for wishing that was what he would say.

He collected his belongings from the tent, giving me a cheery wave as he left for home.

I only saw Bert once more after that. He turned up on the doorstep with a pile of comics that he didn't want to take with him but didn't want to throw away. It was a bit rushed and a bit awkward, he didn't want to come in. He said he still had lots of packing to do, but he'd come round and say goodbye before he went. A part of me suspected that was probably not going to happen, that this would be the last time I would see Bert. I thought I might cry, but I didn't want to do that in front of my friend.

"I'll read them when I come to stay with my old man," he smiled in that easy way of his before turning and striding down the path, pausing at the gate to look over his shoulder and wave before disappearing from my life.

He never did visit, the last time I heard from him was that Christmas, when he sent me a card with a robin on the front. He had drawn a speech bubble coming from the bird's beak and written 'Hi Shorts' in it. Inside the card, it said nothing more than 'Happy Christmas, from Bert'. He had not included his address, so I had no way of returning his greeting.

TWENTY-TWO

"The radio said it's going to rain later," Aunty Jean told Mum as they sat drinking coffee. I didn't take any notice; it didn't seem likely – it hadn't rained since forever, and it was still horribly hot. It was also uncomfortable today; the air was sticky, and the moment I started to do anything that required any sort of effort, it felt like walking through treacle. Even Max wasn't keen on doing anything, staying in the shade at the side of the house with his tongue lolling from the side of his mouth.

I sweated listlessly through the morning and was sitting in my room, lethargically working my way towards the conclusion of The Hobbit. I stopped reading, distracted not by any unusual sound but by the lack of it. It had become eerily quiet, and the gulls had become uncharacteristically silent, there was no traffic noise or sounds of the twins playing in the road; even the house was solemnly hushed. The vacuum left by the lack of the usual background hubbub was suddenly filled - from everywhere and without warning came a deep, ominous rumbling. The far-off boom that concluded the distant drumroll seemed to make the sultry air shake, causing me to put down my book and look out of the window. The road was deserted, and dusty, hot pavements and tarmac were temporarily devoid of any sign of life. Then, as I watched, large dark circles started to appear on the ground, slowly at first, then more and more, until they started to merge. From above me came another noise, the constant and unfamiliar sound of rain pounding onto the roof of the house.

I ran down to the garden and stood in the middle of the lawn, feeling the rain hitting me like miniature darts, then gradually working its way into my hair and seeping through my clothes. I was soon soaked through, with warm water trickling down my upturned face and down my sun-browned back. As I turned to go back inside, another crack of thunder crashed overhead, this time accompanied by a flash of light so bright it turned everything blue momentarily. This caused me to speed up my efforts to get back to the safety and dryness of indoors.

I towelled my hair and changed into dry clothes, then sat watching this wonder of nature as the parched earth greedily sucked down the water that it had been craving all summer. Despite its best efforts, it could not keep up; puddles formed, and drains, blocked with bundles of shrivelled leaves, began to overflow.

And just like that, summer was over. Those seemingly endless days of sunshine in the summer of 1976 would be followed by months of near-continuous rain. What had felt like a magical time that would last forever came to an abrupt end. These final days of the holiday prepared the way for the incoming season that would, in turn, become winter.

Mum made me try on my uniform to make sure it still fit. It was fine. She had made sure that it had 'plenty of growing room' when she had bought it for me. Baggy and long last year, it was now just the right size to grow out of by Christmas. The shoes, trousers and blazer felt unnatural and uncomfortable on my body, which had been unrestricted and unencumbered for the last six weeks.

On the plus side, I found a bag of sherbet pips that I had forgotten about in my pocket. In my dizzy delight at the start of the holiday, I had left them there, and I now retrieved them. They were solidified into one large lump now, of course, with the paper bag stuck firmly to the outer layer. With some careful peeling, followed by a rinse under the tap, I was left with a giant sweet that I could take bites off and eat as I picked the more stubborn shreds of paper from between my teeth.

The last few days disappeared in a blur. Before I knew it, I was parading off back to school, merging into an amorphous sea of uniforms with all the other kids, hundreds of us from all over town. Combined with the countless others being bussed in from the outlying villages, a rag-tag army converged on the sprawling and eclectic mixture of buildings that was our school.

With all the people there, it should have been easy enough for me to find someone who could take Bert's place. But that first week back, I didn't particularly want to try making new friends, everybody else slipped comfortably back into their old cliques and cabals as they gathered to talk about what they had done in the summer, where they had been and what teachers they would be having in the coming year. I sat by myself and wondered what Bert would be doing in his new school. I knew that I didn't want to share everything I had done during the six-week break with anybody.

I was sitting by myself in my busy form room on Friday lunchtime when Theresa came through the door. We weren't supposed to go into other people's form rooms, but it was a rule that was not rigidly enforced and was consequently mostly ignored. She made a beeline for the desk I was sitting at and sat down beside me. She looked different in her school uniform, not as carefree and relaxed as she had in the summer – but still beautiful.

"Did your year group have the assembly?" she asked.

I knew exactly what she meant, and we had. It had been the funeral today. The whole school had been gathered together and asked/told to pay its respects to Clive Williams – or Tubs as everybody, including most of the teachers, knew him. There had been a short speech about how sad it was to lose such a valued member of the school community, which I thought may have been a bit of an exaggeration. I won't say that I didn't feel a bit sad because I did. But that was mostly my feelings of guilt and shame. I wondered what Bert would have made of it.

The thoughts and prayers were followed by a longer missive, warning us of the perils of drinking, smoking and trespassing. This was then rounded off by reminding us of everything we had only just been told but had added helpful information about not getting someone older to buy the drink and cigarettes (which I had never thought of), along with a list of suggested places not to go with our illicit contraband.

"Yes," I answered, "do you think he is going to be sorely missed?"

"Not by me," she grinned. "What are you doing tomorrow?"

"Nothing much."

"Come over to mine. My sister's going next week, she's given me all her records to look after. You can bring Max if you want."

"Okay," my answer may have been a little quick and eager, but I had been sure that Theresa would forget about me once she was back with her friends at school. "How did you know which class I was in anyway?"

She gave me a withering look, "I asked someone," she told me. She smiled, winked and left me sitting at my desk. The girls in the class watched her go, looked at me and began talking in huddles. The boys mostly didn't notice.

AN ENDING

The two men have finally resolved their disagreement about whose turn it is to use the launch ramp, one of their wives has pointed out that there is plenty of room for both of them. They are now busy unloading and sorting out their seafaring paraphernalia, getting ready to set sail.

It could be my imagination, but I think the late afternoon has brought a change in the temperature. It is still uncomfortably hot, but it might feel marginally cooler than it did earlier. It is more likely because I have stopped moving and taken some water on board that I have cooled down, but I am preparing myself for the return trip. I know that my walk back to the car will be as sticky and uncomfortable as my walk here, I half wish I had parked nearer to the seafront.

Nevertheless, I'll soon be walking along my old road, returning to my car and starting my journey back to the normality of everyday life. It's a good life, and I have much to be grateful for; aside from my beautiful family, I have a steady job, a house near the coast and a few close friends. I have worked hard, and life has been kind to me so far. I am still in touch with Theresa (or Taz, as she started to be called the year after I first met her). She lives abroad now; I never told her what Bert said in the tent that night.

I stand and turn my back on the sailors, walking down the beach towards the edge of the seashore. I navigate the towels, bags and people until I arrive at the wet sand, where tiny wavelets brush up towards the toes of my work shoes. Looking out across the estuary, I shield my eyes from the reflections that dance on the tops of the undulating surface, making the sea look like a living thing.

Reaching into my back pocket, I pull out my wallet. It is a rectangle of scuffed and worn brown leather that my children presented to me on Father's Day several years ago. I should probably get a new one soon, but it's not on my to-do list for today. I fumble in the back, amongst the old receipts and business cards, and retrieve a small copper disc. The date, 1964, is still legible. The rest of the old pre-decimal penny is squashed and misshapen, the outline of the queen's head barely visible. I wonder if Bert still has his, although somehow I doubt it.

Holding the coin in my hand, I flex my arm slightly as I prepare to throw it. This is the ritual; I get to this point every time I come here. As I do this, inside my head, I can hear Bert's voice quietly asking,

"What if it wasn't an accident though?"

Was this Bert's confession or his angry fantasy? Part of me still insists on believing that it was an accident; the part of me that doesn't want to share any of the blame. I try my best to block out the memory of those whispered words,

"What if it wasn't an accident though?"

What if….? What if….?

What if we hadn't sent the letter?

What if I hadn't gone with Bert to watch and laugh?

What if I had told someone what I knew?

Life seems to be full of 'what ifs?', increasing in number as the years go by. How do you let them go? The nagging doubts that wake you in the night or pester you in quiet moments? Can we all say that we wouldn't change some things if we had the chance?

The weather today is so like one of those glorious, scorching days in August 1976 that I think today might finally be the day. It could be the day that I leave that summer behind and forgive myself for the part I played in Tub's death and the guilt I felt for not feeling guilty. I can let go of my sadness for the loss of my childhood and my friend. But mostly, it's a day to feel relief that I have made it this far and gratitude for the life that I have had.

My wife and children will be at home, maybe waiting for me, most likely just getting on with mundane and ordinary things, whatever it is they do when I'm not there. My dearest wish for my children is that whatever it is they do when I'm not around, it's not the same stupid things I did when I was a kid. In my heart, I know this is a vain wish because kids do stupid things by default, but even so…

I pull my arm back three times, each time with slightly less conviction than the previous one. I sigh, then carefully return the lucky penny to its place in my battered wallet. Just like every other day I have visited the town, I find myself unable to let go of it, in the same way that I am unable to let go of my memories and all of the what-ifs. The ghosts of my past still hover at my shoulder, following me back through the town. As I always do, I let them walk alongside me, knowing that once I am on the road out of town, I will leave them behind once more – until the next time I find myself here.

Steve Beed was born in 1964. He has three adult children and a beautiful wife. He lives in a small coastal

town in the southwest of England and has published four novels and one novella:

Nothing Happened in 1986

Nothing Else Happened in 2011

Bloglin

Smartphone

King of the Car Park

These can all be found via my author page on Amazon.

You are welcome to write and let me know if you enjoyed this book at:

Stevebeed64@gmail.com

In return, I will add you to my mailing list and let you know about any forthcoming releases.

You can follow my blog at:

https://steevbeed.wordpress.com

Printed in Great Britain
by Amazon